Tallahassee Higgins

Other novels by Mary Downing Hahn

Wait Till Helen Comes
The Jellyfish Season
Daphne's Book
The Time of the Witch
The Sara Summer

Tallahassee
Higgins

MARY DOWNING HAHN

CLARION BOOKS

TICKNOR & FIELDS: A HOUGHTON MIFFLIN COMPANY

New York

Clarion Books
Ticknor & Fields, a Houghton Mifflin Company
Copyright © 1987 by Mary Downing Hahn

Library of Congress Cataloging-in-Publication Data
Hahn, Mary Downing.
Tallahassee Higgins.
Summary: Tallahassee Higgins enjoys the vagabond
lifestyle she lives with her free-spirited mother,
but when Mother goes to Los Angeles to try her luck in
TV and movies, Tallahassee is placed with her uncle, whose
conventional suburban lifestyle makes her question her
mother's values—and her own.
[1. Mothers and daughters—Fiction]   I. Title.
PZ7.H1256Tal   1987   [Fic]   86-17513
ISBN: 0-89919-495-8

A 10 9 8 7 6 5 4 3 2 1

For my daughters, Kate and Beth Hahn,
with love and affection and thanks!

Tallahassee Higgins

Chapter 1

IT WAS FEBRUARY NINTH, 1985, a date I knew I would remember forever as the worst day of my life. My mom and I were sitting in the snack bar at the Miami airport eating hamburgers and waiting for my plane. I was going to Maryland to stay with an uncle and aunt I'd never met, and she was going to California with her boyfriend, Bob.

Liz had several reasons for not taking me. The most obvious was that three people can't ride on a motorcycle. Not even if one of them is a very skinny twelve-year-old girl. I told Bob to get a little sidecar for me, but he said he couldn't afford to waste money on something like that.

To tell you the truth, though, the motorcycle was just part of the problem. Neither Liz nor Bob had the slightest idea what they were going to do when they got to California — they had no jobs out there, no place to live, no real plans. Liz wanted to get into the movies, and Bob claimed he had friends in L.A. who knew people in the film industry. Who they knew Bob never said, which bothered me a lot more than it bothered Liz, who is not the most realistic person you ever met.

"So you're much better off in Hyattsdale with Dan and Thelma," Liz said, reaching for the salt. "As soon as Bob and I get settled, you know, when we have jobs and a place to live and stuff, I'll send you money for a plane ticket."

"When will that be?" I was squeezing my hamburger bun so tightly that the ketchup was dripping out. "A week, two weeks, a month, a year?"

Liz tossed her long, golden hair over her shoulders and shook her head. "Oh, not a year, Tallahassee," she said. "Maybe a month or two. I just don't know, honey."

She lit a cigarette and puffed the smoke straight up so it wouldn't blow in my face. "Anyway, we need a break from each other, don't you think? After all, it's been just the two of us for twelve years."

I forced myself to swallow a mouthful of dry hamburger. "I don't need a break from you," I mumbled. "You're my mother, and I love you."

"Well, I love you too, Tinkerbell." Liz laughed and ruffled my hair. "Silly old carrottop — love's not the issue here."

Ducking away from her hand, I turned to the window and watched a jet roll down the runway. I didn't like it when Liz turned serious things into jokes. "Don't call me carrottop. Or Tinkerbell," I said.

"Oh, Talley, quit pouting." Liz tried to pat my hand,

but I snatched it away. "It'll be good for you to have a little stability. You and me, we've been living like gypsies for so long, honey, but Dan and Thelma can give you a real home for a while."

"I like the way me and you live." It was true. We never had much money, but I didn't care.

"Maybe you do, but I don't." Liz sipped her diet soda. "I'm sick of going from one waitress job to another and living in crummy apartments, never knowing how I'm going to pay the rent, worrying about tips, worrying about you all alone at night."

She leaned across the table, forcing me to look at her. "Don't you see, honey? This is my chance to get out of this rut while I'm still young, before I lose my looks. Bob's sure his friends can get me into the movies. Don't make it so hard for me, Tallahassee!"

"If I could just go with you, Liz." Even though I was trying hard not to whine, I could hear my voice rising.

"You'll like Hyattsdale, honest you will." Liz smiled at me. "Just think, honey," she went on, "you'll sleep in my old room and go to my old school, and you'll love Dan. He's the best big brother in the world."

I chewed a mouthful of ice from my soda to keep myself from saying what I was thinking — if Uncle Dan was so wonderful, why had Liz run away when she was only seventeen years old? And why hadn't she ever gone back to see him?

"He was like a father to me after our parents died," Liz said softly. "I wasn't much older than you, Tallahassee, and Dan was twenty-four or twenty-five. He was still living at home and working at the phone company, saving his money to marry Thelma." She sipped her diet soda. "Good old Dan, solid as a rock."

I'd heard all this a million times before, of course, but it still made me sad that my grandparents had been killed in a plane crash before I was even born. I would have liked to have known them. As far as I knew, I didn't have any other grandparents. Or a father, for that matter, since Liz had never told me anything about him. Not even his name.

"Dan just can't wait to meet you, Tallahassee." Liz patted my hand and smiled at me, bringing me back to the snack bar.

"How about Aunt Thelma?" I crushed my empty soda cup while I waited for Liz to answer. I knew perfectly well how she felt about Aunt Thelma. "I'll bet she can't wait either," I added, trying to sound as sarcastic as possible.

"I'm sure Thelma will be very nice to you," Liz said stiffly.

"But she won't like me."

Liz sighed and ground out her cigarette. "Thelma and I didn't get along, you know that, but she hasn't seen me for over twelve years. And you're just a kid. She won't hold a grudge against you, honey."

Silently, I watched Liz light another cigarette. As she exhaled, I leaned toward her. "I thought you were going to cut down on cigarettes," I said.

"Don't nag me, Tallahassee." Liz frowned at me through a cloud of smoke. "I'm a little tense right now, but as soon as I get out to California, I'm going to quit. I promise."

"You'll get wrinkles if you keep on smoking like that," I told her. "Not to mention lung cancer and emphysema. The way you cough in the morning, I bet your lungs are all black." I stared at her. "And you're already getting little teeny lines on your upper lip."

"Will you quit telling me things like that?" Liz glared at me. "It's not true, anyway. About the wrinkles." She touched her mouth nervously.

I slid lower in my seat and poked at the remains of my hamburger. Without me to take care of her, I really didn't know how Liz was going to survive. That might sound weird, considering that she's the adult and I'm the kid, but she just doesn't have any sense. I'd been helping her manage money and fix meals for years, and I wasn't sure that Bob was going to do nearly as good a job. Most of the time he looked like he was walking in his sleep.

"Are you sure you're going to have enough money for food and gas?" I asked Liz. "It's a long way to California, and you have to go through a desert to get there."

"Tallahassee, will you stop nagging me?" Liz stubbed out her cigarette. "I'm an adult. I know how to take care of myself."

"But what if you get depressed? Who'll cheer you

up?" I asked. "I bet Bob can't walk on his hands like me or tell knock-knock jokes."

Liz looked at her watch. "We'd better go, Talley," she said. "Your plane leaves in about twenty minutes."

"Can Bob do Ginger Rogers and Fred Astaire dances like you and me? Does he have a Glinda the Good Witch Magic Wand to wave over your head?" I was close to tears as I followed Liz through the maze of little tables crowded with travelers.

"Will you shut up?" Liz frowned at me. "You're embarrassing me, Tallahassee Higgins."

"But I'm so worried about you!" When I tried to take her hand, she yanked it away, her face red.

"Here comes Bob to see you off," Liz said. "Don't let him see you acting like a baby."

Wiping my eyes with the back of my hand, I shifted my backpack to my shoulders and watched Bob ambling down the corridor toward us, carrying a big plastic bag. He was wearing his usual faded jeans and a new T-shirt that said, California, Here I Come.

After giving Liz a big hug, Bob smiled at me. "Hi, kid," he said. "This is for you."

To my surprise, he pulled a box out of the bag and handed it to me. It was wrapped in pretty paper and tied with a big, pink bow. "Don't open it now," he said. "Save it for after you get on the plane."

"What is it?"

"A surprise." He grinned so widely I thought his face might split. "Your mom helped me pick it out."

As he and Liz started kissing again, I shook the box.

Something slid softly back and forth inside. It sounded like a stuffed animal, I thought, and I remembered the beautiful white bear Liz and I had seen at the Seaway Mall. Liz had said that nobody in his right mind would pay eighty dollars for a teddy bear, but here it was, I was sure of it, a special going-away present from her and Bob.

I turned to Liz to thank her, but she was laughing at something Bob had said. For all the attention I was getting, I might as well have been in Maryland. Grabbing Liz's hand, I squeezed it as hard as I could.

"Don't you even care that you're not going to see me for a long time?" I yelled. "You'll be alone with him all the way to California. Can't you at least *look* at me?" Tears smarted in my eyes, but I didn't care if every nosy person in the whole world saw me crying.

"Oh, Talley, for goodness' sake, honey!" Liz pulled her hand free and hugged me. "Don't be such a silly baby!"

"You will miss me, won't you?"

"I'll send you a postcard every day, I promise, sweetie." Her perfume enclosed me in a fragrant cloud and her hair tumbled down around me, curtaining me from the people rushing past. "It's just for a little while, honey, that's all." Liz was crying now, too, but she straightened up when she heard the loudspeaker announcing my flight.

"Come on, you two," Bob said. "We don't want to miss the plane."

Although I tried to delay things by dropping first my

backpack and then my present, Liz and Bob hustled me toward the line of people waiting to board the flight to Washington.

"Be good, honey," Liz whispered in my ear, "and give Dan my love. I'll see you soon. I promise, Talley, I promise."

Then she stepped back, and I followed a fat man into the plane. Although I had a seat by the window, I was on the side facing the runway instead of the airport, so I couldn't wave at Liz. Closing my eyes, I gripped the package Bob had given me and tried not to cry as the plane rolled down the runway, picked up speed, and roared up into the sky.

Chapter 2

THE NEXT TIME I looked out the window, the houses and roads were like a model railroad village far below me. I had never been on an airplane, and I felt very grown-up when the flight attendant stopped her little cart by my seat and asked me what I wanted to drink. I chose a root beer and sipped it slowly as the clouds floated past below me. Was Liz down there somewhere watching the plane vanish? Or was she already heading out to California on the mother stealer's motorcycle, glad to be rid of me?

Just as I was about to cry, I remembered the present Bob had given me. Reaching into my backpack, I pulled out the box and yanked off the ribbon and paper. Inside, instead of a beautiful white bear, I saw an ugly doll smiling up at me. She had a round face and orange hair, sort of like mine, and her two fat arms were reaching up for me.

"Oh, isn't she adorable!" One of the flight attendants leaned over the man next to me to get a better look at the hideous creature. "She even has her own birth certificate, doesn't she?"

I looked at the slip of paper in the box. It said the doll's name was Melanie. Melon Head was more like it.

"My little niece is just dying to have one of those. Aren't you lucky?" the flight attendant gushed.

I frowned at Melon Head. "I'm twelve years old," I said. "I haven't played with dolls for years."

The man beside me glanced at the open box. "My wife has a whole collection of those little monsters. Ugly as sin, aren't they?" He winked at me and poked his nose back into *The Wall Street Journal.*

"Oh, how can you say such a thing!" The flight attendant giggled in a flirty way that reminded me of Liz, but when the man just shrugged and kept on reading, she walked off down the aisle, looking for people who were more fun.

I frowned at Melon Head. Her face was all scrunched up from her dopey smile, and she looked like an idiot. Why couldn't she have been that beautiful white bear? Closing the lid so I wouldn't have to see her, I shut my eyes and pretended to be asleep all the way to Washington.

*

When I got off the airplane, I looked for Uncle Dan. According to Liz, he was around forty, tall, and probably kind of fat. "His hair was brown the last time I saw him," she had added, "but it's probably gray now. He might even be bald."

At least half the men I saw matched Liz's description, but as far as I could tell, I was the only red-headed girl in the whole airport. Hoping I would be easy to find, I stood in the middle of the waiting area and watched all the other passengers rush into the arms of their friends and relatives.

Just as I was beginning to think Aunt Thelma had told Uncle Dan not to come, I saw a tall man walking toward me. He was smiling a little uncertainly, and his eyes were gray-green like Liz's.

"Are you Tallahassee Higgins?" I nodded. He smiled Liz's smile and added, "I'm your Uncle Dan."

I wanted to run to him and give him a big hug, but I was scared. He didn't know me, not really, and I didn't know him. Maybe he didn't like hugs — how did I know? So I just stood there, gawking at him, too nervous even to smile.

"I'm sorry I'm late," he said. "I got held up in a traffic jam on the Beltway. A tractor trailer truck blew a tire and spilled lumber all over the place."

"That's okay." I gripped Melanie's box as if she were the only thing left in the world. "The plane was late, too."

"Where's your luggage?" Uncle Dan looked around, as if he were expecting to see more than my backpack.

"This is all I have," I said.

"Well, let me take it." Uncle Dan's big hand closed around the strap of my backpack. "What's in the box?"

"Oh, just a dumb old doll Bob gave me." I eyed a trash can, wondering what Uncle Dan would do if I tossed Melanie into it.

"Dumb old doll, huh?" Uncle Dan chuckled. "You sound just like your mom. She never cared much for dolls either."

When we got to the door, I felt a freezing blast of air, and Uncle Dan said, "You'd better get your coat on, Tallahassee. It's cold outside."

I looked up at him. "I don't have a coat," I said. "I never needed one in Florida."

"But you're in Maryland now, Tallahassee. Surely Liz hasn't forgotten how cold it is in February."

"I've got something in my backpack." I rummaged through my clothes and pulled out an old Miami Dolphins sweatshirt. Yanking it over my head, I followed Uncle Dan outside. It was dark, and the wind felt like it was blowing straight out of the North Pole. Why hadn't Liz told me I was going to the Arctic? With my head down, I ran to Uncle Dan's pickup truck.

"Can I ride in the back?" I already had one leg over the side, sure he'd say yes.

"Of course not. Do you want to get killed?"

"What do you mean? Liz's old boyfriend, Roger, always let me ride in the back of his truck, and nothing ever happened to me." I stared at Uncle Dan, too surprised to give him much of an argument.

"Have you ever thought what would happen to you if I had to slam on my brakes?" He opened the passenger door. "Come on, Tallahassee, get in here before you freeze to death."

Thinking he was probably right about freezing, I slid

onto the seat beside him. Maybe when the weather got warmer, I'd be able to talk him into letting me ride in the back. But of course I wouldn't be here then, I reminded myself. I'd be out in California riding the waves on my surfboard.

"Well, how is your mom, Tallahassee?" Uncle Dan glanced at me as he nosed the truck into the flow of traffic leaving the airport.

"Oh, she's fine," I told him. "She's going to be a famous movie star."

"She is?" Uncle Dan stared at me.

"Bob has connections in Hollywood. You know, friends in the film industry. They're going to help her."

"I didn't know Liz had any training in acting," Uncle Dan said.

"Bob says she has natural talent." I leaned toward Uncle Dan, trying to convince him as well as myself that Liz was doing the right thing. "She was a waitress in this big dinner theater in Tampa, the kind where the whole staff sings in the chorus, and Bob was working in the sound booth. When he saw Liz, he was just sure she could make it in Hollywood. He says she has the looks and the talent."

"But Hollywood?" Uncle Dan looked doubtful. "It's not easy to get into the movies."

"Liz is so beautiful, I just know she'll be a star in no time," I said. "And then you can tell everybody you're her big brother. You'll be famous, too. *People* magazine might even interview you or something." I smiled at him, feeling a little more relaxed now that I was getting to know him better.

"Is Bob a nice fellow?" Uncle Dan asked.

"He's okay, I guess, but I liked some of Liz's other boyfriends better. Especially Roger, the one who let me ride in the back of his truck. He wanted to marry her, but she didn't want to stay in Florida for the rest of her life."

"I sure wish Liz could have come with you," Uncle Dan said. "I'd love to see her again."

He sighed, and neither of us said anything for a few minutes. Like my uncle, I wished with all my heart that Liz were sitting here in the truck with us. She seemed so far away, lost in the night, cruising along with Bob on a road I'd never seen.

"Your Aunt Thelma and I are delighted about having you with us, Tallahassee," Uncle Dan said finally. "You're our one and only niece. That makes you pretty special."

"Really?" I glanced at him, but he was looking straight ahead, concentrating on the traffic around us.

"Look over there," he said, pointing to the left. "We're crossing the Potomac River. See the Capitol and the Washington Monument? Aren't they pretty all lit up?"

I stared across the river, almost unable to believe I was seeing the most famous building in America. "They look like a movie set," I said. "Are they really real?"

Uncle Dan nodded. "Some Saturday, Thelma and I

will bring you down to see the sights. We could go to the museums, too. Would you like that?"

"I guess so." I turned my head and watched the Washington skyline disappear behind us. "If we have time," I told him. "I won't be here very long, you know."

*

When we got to Hyattsdale, I was half-asleep, my head bobbing against Uncle Dan's shoulder.

"We're almost home, Tallahassee." Uncle Dan stopped at a red light. "This is Farragut Street," he said as he turned off Route One. "We live on Oglethorpe, right on the corner."

Pressing my nose against the window, I stared at the houses we were passing. Most of them were big and old-fashioned. They sat back from the street, surrounded by huge yards and bushes and tall trees. Some had towers on the side, and others had cupolas on the roof. Almost all of them had big front porches that made you think of old-fashioned summer days and ladies in long dresses sipping lemonade.

Here and there, stuck in between the big houses, were bungalows with dormered roofs and ramblers with picture windows. Most of them had swing sets in the yard and bicycles on the porch. They didn't make you think of anything except kids and dogs and boring suburban stuff.

Although I was hoping that Uncle Dan lived in a big house with a tower, he pulled into a driveway beside a plain gray bungalow and turned off the engine. "Here we are, Tallahassee," he said. "Let's get inside fast. Thelma's got a nice, hot dinner ready for us."

Clutching my door handle, I watched Uncle Dan walk around the front of the truck. The wind was thumping against the windows, but it wasn't just the cold that made me reluctant to open the door. In a few seconds I was going to come face to face with Aunt Thelma — the old grump, as Liz called her — and I felt like a little kid being sent to the principal's office. You know how that is — your insides are all tied up in knots, your mouth is dry, your legs shake because you know the principal isn't going to be happy to see you. She isn't going to like you.

"Come on, honey." Uncle Dan opened the door and took my arm to help me out of the truck. "We're home."

Shivering as the wind blasted my face, I let my uncle lead me up the walk toward the house that could never be home for me without Liz.

Chapter 3

Aunt Thelma was standing at the front door, waiting for us. She was short and plump, and her hair was a sort of artificial reddish blonde. Although she smiled at me, the little dog beside her barked fiercely.

"Hush, Fritzi." She picked up the dog, who continued to snarl at me. He was brown and white, and he had a pointed face. Like Aunt Thelma, he was kind of overweight.

"Well, well, so here you are, Tallahassee." Aunt Thelma said my name as if it were a foreign word, and when I moved toward her, thinking she might want to hug me, she stepped back into the house without even trying to touch me.

"I'll bet you're hungry," she said, leading us down a dark hall to the dining room. "They never give you enough food on an airplane."

"I didn't have anything except a bag of honey-roasted

nuts and a root beer," I said. "Only first class got a meal."

"Well, I've got a nice stew all ready for you. Just sit down, and I'll have our plates ready in a jiffy."

I took the chair sitting by itself on one side of the table, and Uncle Dan sat at the head of the table. In the silence we could hear Aunt Thelma rattling things in the kitchen. Fritzi had followed her out there, but he was keeping an eye on me from the doorway. He growled very softly when he saw me looking at him.

"Usually dogs like me," I said to Uncle Dan.

"Oh, don't pay any attention to Fritzi," he replied. "Children make him nervous."

"I'm not a child," I said. "I'm an adolescent."

"Here comes dinner," he said.

Aunt Thelma put plates in front of Uncle Dan and me and brought one more for herself.

Taking an enormous bite out of a biscuit, Uncle Dan turned to me. "I hope you brought your appetite with you, Tallahassee. Thelma's just about the best cook in the world."

"Liz is a good cook, too," I said, which was a lie. For years we had lived on frozen pizzas and Quarter Pounders from McDonald's.

Aunt Thelma smiled at me. "I'm so glad Liz finally met a nice man. It's about time she settled down."

"Settle down?" I swallowed a mouthful of stew. "Liz will never settle down."

"She's going to marry this man, isn't she?" Aunt Thelma's face reddened slightly.

"I *hope* not." I thought of Liz and Bob married, living in a boring little house, maybe having a baby or something. "Liz doesn't ever want to get married. She'd never trap herself that way."

Aunt Thelma and Uncle Dan looked at each other. When they didn't say anything, I added, "She says men always end up expecting you to wash their shirts and do the ironing and cook dinner every night. Liz could never do that."

The only sound was the *click, click* of Fritzi's toenails on the kitchen floor, and I had a feeling I must have said something wrong. Scooping up a big forkful of stew, I busied myself chewing while Aunt Thelma stared at me, her mouth too full of biscuit to say anything.

Uncle Dan turned to her. "Tallahassee tells me Liz is hoping to get into the movies. This fellow Bob knows some people in the film industry. Isn't that right?" He smiled at me, inviting me to help channel the conversation into safer waters.

"She's going to be a big star," I told Aunt Thelma proudly. "Bob says she has the looks and the talent."

"Really?" Aunt Thelma shot Uncle Dan a look. "Remember how she used to go into Washington and play her guitar at Dupont Circle? That's where all the trouble started."

Uncle Dan shifted his position as if his chair had suddenly gotten uncomfortable. "Liz had a lovely voice," he said a little stiffly.

"No training, though. No discipline." Aunt Thelma

took a forkful of stew, chewed it thoughtfully, and turned to me. "How about you, Tallahassee? Do you sing?"

"Liz says I'm just like my father — the only way I can carry a tune is in a bucket." As they exchanged another glance, something occurred to me. "Did you ever meet him? My father?"

I laid down my fork, anxious to hear what they had to say. All my life my father had been a mystery to me. Whenever I'd asked Liz about him, she'd laughed and made up stories. Sometimes she told me he was a dangerous criminal, a drug dealer, or a bank robber. Other times he was a count from a foreign country or a circus clown. Once in a while he was just an ordinary person, too boring to talk about. All I really knew was that he had red hair and big teeth like mine, and he couldn't sing.

Uncle Dan bent his head over his plate and busied himself sopping up gravy with his biscuit, but Aunt Thelma shook her head. "Liz left here before you were born, Tallahassee."

In the silence following her answer, the clock on the living-room wall chimed and the wind rattled the windowpanes. But as I looked from one to the other, I was sure they knew more than they were saying. I swallowed the last mouthful of stew and promised myself that I would poke and pry till I found out what they were hiding.

"My, it sounds like it's getting cold out there." Aunt

Thelma shivered and drew her sweater a little tighter. "How about dessert?" she asked. "I baked a nice cherry pie just for you, Tallahassee."

When we were finished, Aunt Thelma turned to me. "You've had a long day. I imagine you're ready for bed."

I started to argue with her. After all, it was only eight-thirty, and I usually stayed up as late as I liked. But I was exhausted — not just from the trip but from having to talk all night with strangers. The kind of conversation we'd been having can really wear a person out.

Saying good-night to Uncle Dan, I picked up my box and my backpack and followed Aunt Thelma upstairs.

Chapter 4

"**T**HIS IS LIZ'S old room." Aunt Thelma opened a door at the end of the hall, letting a wave of cold air rush past us. "It's pretty much as she left it. Dan never had the heart to clean it out."

I looked past her, at the pictures of horses tacked all over the walls. Some were cut from magazines, but most of them were hand drawn.

"When Liz was your age, she was totally horse crazy," Aunt Thelma said. "Then she discovered boys."

"Really?" I examined some of Liz's drawings. In every school I'd ever gone to, there was always a girl who drew horses. It was funny to think that here in Hyattsdale Liz had been that girl.

"Do you like horses?" Aunt Thelma turned to me, her eyes probing mine. What she really wanted to ask, I was sure, was "Are you just like your mother?"

I was tempted to tell her that I had skipped horses and gone straight to boys, but it wouldn't have been true. Instead, I shrugged my shoulders. "They're all right, I guess." Actually, I'd never thought much about horses, one way or the other.

Aunt Thelma contemplated the pictures silently for a moment. Then she cleared her throat and turned to me. "Tallahassee, I want to make a few things clear right from the start," she began, as if she were delivering a speech she had rehearsed, and I braced myself for bad news.

"While you are here with us, I expect you to obey Dan and me and to do what we tell you. I don't know what kind of life you led in Florida, but *here* we have rules."

While she droned on and on about bedtimes and television and keeping my room clean, I stared uncomfortably at the little hooked rug on the floor. Liz had never cared when I went to bed or how much TV I watched or what my room looked like. Usually I didn't even have a room — I slept on the couch or something. The more Aunt Thelma said, the worse Hyattsdale sounded, and I hoped I wouldn't have to stay long. Otherwise, I was sure I'd end up running away, just like Liz.

"I want your visit to be a pleasant experience for all of us." Aunt Thelma finally stopped talking and turned down the bedspread. Fluffing up the pillow, she said, "You get a good night's sleep now, Tallahassee."

She paused in the doorway as if she were going to say something else. Changing her mind, she gave me a tiny smile and went back downstairs.

Alone in Liz's cold little room, I opened my backpack and pulled out my nightgown. While I undressed, I studied Liz's horses. Their heads were too big, I decided, and their legs were too long. In real life, they wouldn't have been able to walk without falling down, but most of them were leaping over fences, manes and tails flowing in the wind. Despite their anatomical problems, they had a lot of life and spirit, I thought, kind of like Liz herself.

Before I got into bed, I glanced at Melanie's box. It was sitting on the bureau, its lid slightly askew. Opening it, I picked Melanie up.

"Still smiling, Melon Head?" I gave her a little shake. "If you had any brains at all, you'd be bawling your head off."

I started to toss her back into the box, but she was still smiling and holding her arms out as if she expected to be loved. "Oh, okay," I told her. "You can sleep with me. But just tonight, stupid. Don't start thinking I *like* you or anything."

Shivering in my cold bed, I wondered where Liz was now. Would she still be in Florida or would she be in Mississippi already? For the first time in my whole life, I wished I'd paid more attention in geography. Maybe Uncle Dan had a map, I thought, and he'd let me put little thumbtacks in it every time I got a postcard from Liz. That way, I could imagine being in all the places she was passing through on the mother stealer's motorcycle.

*

The first time you go to sleep in a strange place, every little noise wakes you up. First it was Fritzi's toenails out in the hall, then it was a train whistle, then it was Uncle Dan's and Aunt Thelma's voices coming right through the wall between our rooms.

"She has to know who's boss, right from the start," I heard Aunt Thelma say. "Otherwise we'll have another Liz on our hands. I'm forty years old, Dan, and I can't go through that again. It was bad enough the first time."

"Tallahassee seems like a real nice kid," Uncle Dan rumbled. "That smile of hers reminds me so much of Liz. And some of her mannerisms. Did you notice the way she flips her hair out of her face? It was like seeing Liz all over again at that age."

"That's just it, Dan. We don't want Liz all over again! You thought she was a nice kid, too, and look how she turned out. Almost thirty and still acting like a teenager. Riding off to California on a motorcycle to be a movie star. How immature can you get?"

"I don't see any harm in it, Thelma. Liz has so much talent. If anybody can make it out there, she can."

"She has responsibilities, Dan. And if she doesn't shoulder them, who will?" Aunt Thelma's voice was rising. "You and me, Dan, that's who! I knew when Tallahassee was born we'd end up raising her. I'm just surprised it took this long."

"Having her here for a little visit is hardly what I'd call raising her."

"Do you really think Liz will send for her?" Aunt Thelma asked loudly. "I'll be surprised if we ever hear from your sister again!"

"Hush, Thelma. You'll wake up Tallahassee." Uncle Dan's voice dropped, and I heard the bed creak.

Then Aunt Thelma said in a softer voice, "I just don't want Liz to take advantage of you, Dan. I don't want her breaking your heart all over again."

I lay still, wanting to hear more, but — at the same time — wishing I hadn't heard any of it. On the wall opposite me, Liz's horses glimmered in the faint light, and I shivered, feeling cold all the way to my bones. Suppose Aunt Thelma was right and Liz was gone for good? California was a big state, and she hadn't given me an address. Just a promise that she'd write to me every day.

Holding Melanie tight, I remembered our old cat, Bilbo. Liz had always claimed to love him, but when she started dating a guy who hated cats, Bilbo conveniently disappeared. She claimed she didn't know where he'd gone, but I suspected she'd taken him somewhere in the car and dumped him far away while I was in school.

It wouldn't have been so bad if she had at least missed Bilbo. But she didn't. Not a bit. "What's gone is gone," she used to say whenever I asked her about him. "Out of sight, out of mind."

It was the same with the boyfriends she'd had before she met Bob — even Roger, who used to take us snorkeling and waterskiing every weekend. Once she broke up with them, she never thought of them again.

Lying there hugging Melanie, I wondered if Liz would forget about me. I could just see her walking along a beach somewhere in California, laughing and talking, never even wondering how I was doing. Then she would receive a telegram from Aunt Thelma telling her I had died of pneumonia. She would stare at the message. "Tallahassee?" she would ask herself. "I don't know anybody named Tallahassee. I thought that was a city, not a *person*." Then she would shrug, crumple the telegram into a ball, and toss it into the Pacific.

Chapter 5

AUNT THELMA WOKE me up on Saturday morning. "It's almost nine-thirty," she said. "And we need to go shopping."

I huddled under the covers. "Me and Liz always sleep late on Saturdays," I said, not even bothering to smile at her or even sound nice. I knew how she felt about me now. And Liz, too.

"What did I tell you last night about rules?" Aunt Thelma sounded just as grumpy as I felt. "I expect you to be up and dressed by nine o'clock on weekends." She folded her arms across her chest and frowned like a prison matron in an old movie.

When I didn't move, she yanked the covers off, tumbling poor old Melanie to the floor and exposing me to the cold air. "Get dressed right this minute. Your breakfast is on the table, and your uncle and I are ready to go to the mall."

I jumped out of bed shivering and glared at her. "Why do we have to go to the mall?"

"You don't have any winter clothes, not even a jacket. I can't send you off to school with nothing to wear but those skimpy little things you brought with you from Florida."

"If my mother thought I'd need warm clothes, she'd have gotten them for me!" I felt tears springing to my eyes, so I yelled to keep her from noticing. "I heard every word you said about me and Liz last night, and no matter what you think, she's a very responsible person. I'll only be here a little while, so don't waste your money on clothes for me! I won't need them in California!"

Aunt Thelma's face turned a deep red. "Don't you dare sass me, Tallahassee Higgins! I won't put up with it!"

"What's going on?" Uncle Dan paused in the doorway and looked from me to Aunt Thelma and back again.

"Just tell her to get dressed." Aunt Thelma turned away, her shoulders square, her back straight. "We have to go shopping. She can't run around here in summer clothes."

As she clumped heavily down the steps, Uncle Dan put his arm around my shoulders and gave me a little hug. "You must be freezing to death, honey. Get dressed before you catch pneumonia or something."

"She hates me," I sobbed. "She hates me and Liz."

"You heard us talking last night, didn't you?" Uncle Dan asked softly.

I nodded and hid my face in my hands. I hardly ever cry and I hate people to see me when I do. "But it's not true," I sobbed. "Liz would never go off and leave me."

"Of course she wouldn't, honey." Uncle Dan patted my head. "Your aunt gets all riled up sometimes and talks nonsense. She had no business scaring you like that." He offered me his handkerchief. "Stop crying now and forget all about it. Okay?"

After Uncle Dan left, I picked up Melanie. "Liz will send for me in just a few weeks, I bet," I whispered to her. "She'll miss me so much she'll get all sad, and Bob won't know how to cheer her up the way I do."

I pulled my Glinda the Good Witch Magic Wand out of my backpack. The stick was bent and the star was crooked, but I waved it through the air and tapped Melanie lightly on the head. "Be happy," I crooned, and then I swooped around the room on my toes.

Unlike Liz, Melanie didn't laugh at my Glinda routine, but she looked happy. Picking her up, I gave her a little shake and made her say, "Liz loves you more than anything in the whole world, Tallahassee Higgins. You're the only person who can make her truly happy."

Sitting Melanie on the bureau, I rummaged through the stuff in my backpack, trying to find some underpants that didn't have holes in them. I only had four pairs, and all of them were the Sunday kind — holy. Hoping Aunt Thelma wouldn't follow me into the dressing room at the mall, I put on the least raggedy ones, yanked on my jeans and a T-shirt, and ran downstairs.

Fritzi was waiting for me in the hall, growling like a killer dog. I tried to walk around him, but he blocked my path and snarled.

"Nice dog, nice dog." I stretched my hand toward him the way Liz had taught me. "Let them smell you," she always said, "so they'll know you aren't threatening them."

I guess the message didn't get through because Fritzi continued to growl and then to bark — sharp, loud yapping sounds.

"Tallahassee, leave that dog alone." Aunt Thelma stepped into the hall and picked Fritzi up. Kissing his nose, she said, "Come on, sweetie, I'll give you a puppy bone."

"I wasn't doing anything to him," I told her. "For your information, he was trying to bite me. Are you sure he doesn't have rabies or something?"

When she didn't answer, I stuck my tongue out at Fritzi, who was growling at me over Aunt Thelma's shoulder.

"Sit down and eat, Tallahassee." Aunt Thelma put a bowl on the table next to a glass of orange juice. "We haven't got all day."

"What's this?" I poked at the warm gray stuff in the bowl, thinking she must have given me Fritzi's food by mistake.

"Haven't you ever eaten oatmeal?" she asked coldly. Neither of us had forgotten the scene we'd had upstairs, and the air in the kitchen was heavy with unspoken words.

I looked at the cup she was holding. "I'll just have coffee." I tried to sound as cold as she had.

"Coffee?" Aunt Thelma couldn't have looked more shocked if I'd asked for a beer. "Coffee is for adults, not children. You eat that oatmeal, Tallahassee. Breakfast is the most important meal of the day."

Sitting down across from me, she put her cup on the table. I could see the steam curling up from it and smell the good coffee aroma. Then she opened the newspaper to the crossword puzzle, picked up a pencil, and started filling in the blanks.

I don't know how long we would have sat there if Uncle Dan hadn't come through the back door, huffing from the cold. "Are you two ready?" he asked.

"When Tallahassee finishes her breakfast," Aunt Thelma said.

"I told her all I wanted was coffee, but she won't even let me have one cup." I glared at Aunt Thelma, but she had her head bent over the crossword puzzle as if it were the most important thing in the world.

Uncle Dan looked at my oatmeal. "It's cold, Thelma. Maybe you should give her cornflakes instead."

Aunt Thelma shot him a dirty look, but she poured some cornflakes into a bowl and put it down in front of me. Then, sighing loudly, she dumped the oatmeal in the garbage disposal.

After I'd eaten enough to satisfy her, I pulled on my sweatshirt and followed them outside to Aunt Thelma's car, an old Ford. I got into the back seat, which smelled like Fritzi, and Uncle Dan struggled to start the engine.

"Roger's truck used to sound just like this," I told Uncle Dan. "He said it was because it needed a new choke."

Uncle Dan nodded and Aunt Thelma muttered something about not knowing I was an automobile mechanic. Finally, the car started and we set off for the mall.

*

By the time Aunt Thelma had finished dragging me from one store to another looking for sales, I had a green and blue ski jacket, a new pair of jeans, and three sweaters, plus socks, underwear, and mittens. I hated to think of how much money Aunt Thelma had wasted, but I promised her that Liz would pay her back. "Every cent," I said. "Even though I don't need any of these clothes."

On the way back to Oglethorpe Street, we passed a McDonald's. "Can we eat dinner there?" I leaned over the seat, addressing my request to Uncle Dan.

"Certainly not." Aunt Thelma reared her head back like an angry horse. "You had a hot dog at the mall. That's enough junk food for one day."

In my opinion you can never have enough junk food, but I knew better than to try telling Aunt Thelma that. Instead I slumped in the backseat and wondered what Liz was doing. Ten to one, she and the mother stealer were eating Big Macs somewhere.

*

After dinner Aunt Thelma and I had one more fight. This time it was about television. I wanted to stay up and watch *The Bride of Dracula* on *Creature Feature*, but Aunt Thelma reminded me that my bedtime was nine-thirty on weekends.

"You certainly can't stay up until two in the morning watching a horror film," she said.

"Liz lets me see anything I want." I glared at Aunt Thelma. "And she never makes me go to bed."

I'm sure Aunt Thelma thought I was lying, but I wasn't. I'd been watching horror films all my life, partly because Liz was scared to watch them by herself. And I'd always stayed up till I fell asleep, usually on the floor in front of the television set. Then Liz would carry me to bed.

"Well, you aren't living with Liz now." Aunt Thelma turned off the television, right in the middle of an old *Fantasy Island* rerun. "So go on upstairs before I lose my temper."

"Can't I at least watch the end of *Fantasy Island?*" I asked. "It's one of my favorites. This woman is going to drink from the fountain of youth — that's her wish — and then she's going to find out it's really awful to see everybody you love get old while you stay young, and the dwarf is going — "

"That's enough, Tallahassee," Aunt Thelma rudely interrupted me. "If you know the show so well, you don't need to see it again."

"But I don't remember all of it," I said. "I forget how it ends. There's always this twist, you know, and — "

Aunt Thelma put her hands on my shoulders and turned me toward the stairs. "Go to bed," she said. "This minute!"

"You hate me!" I yelled at her as Uncle Dan came up from the basement. "You hate Liz and you hate me!"

"You do something with her," Aunt Thelma said to Uncle Dan. "I can't put up with this behavior."

"All I wanted to do was stay up and see *The Bride of Dracula*," I told Uncle Dan, "but she won't even let me watch *Fantasy Island*."

"You be a good girl and do what your aunt tells you, Tallahassee," Uncle Dan said gently as Aunt Thelma stalked off to the kitchen with Fritzi at her heels. "You know it's your bedtime."

I opened my mouth to argue, but Uncle Dan just shook his head. "Go on, now," he said.

Unhappily, I went to my room, undressed, and got into bed with Melanie. "Well," I whispered, "things aren't getting any better, are they?"

"I hope Liz sends the money for your ticket soon," I made Melanie say. "Or we'll both go nuts."

Holding silly old Melon Head in my arms, I stared at the shadows on the ceiling and thought up stories about the shapes they made. If I looked real hard, I could see Liz and Bob riding on a motorcycle right over my head. Liz's hair blew around her face, almost hiding it, but I knew she was thinking about me, feeling lonely for me, wishing I was there to do a little dance for her or tell her a new knock-knock joke.

Chapter 6

SUNDAY WAS A GRAY DAY, full of rain and wind.
I managed to avoid Aunt Thelma by spending most
of the afternoon in Liz's room, reading her old horse
books and worrying about school. What were kids like
in Maryland? My clothes, my hair, my accent — everything about me might be weird. Suppose they laughed
at me? Suppose nobody wanted to be friends with me?

Before I went to sleep that night, I had a long talk
with Melanie. "I've gone to ten schools," I told her,
"because Liz never likes to stay in one place for more
than a few months. And I've only had about three
friends in my whole life, but it never mattered because
I had Liz. Now I'm all by myself."

I hugged Melanie and stared at Liz's horses gallop-
ing across the flowered wallpaper. "Do you think anybody will like me?" I asked Melanie.

"Of course they will," I made her say. She was very
loyal. "All the girls will want to sit next to you at lunch
and the boys will fall madly in love with you."

I was sure that all the knock-knock jokes I knew wouldn't impress her; she would have already heard every one of them.

"I never met anybody named Tallahassee before," Dawn said as she led me down a long hall. "I always thought that was a city, not a person's name."

I stared at the tan tiles under my feet and wished Dawn hadn't zeroed in on my name first thing. It was so embarrassing, and I'd never quite forgiven Liz. Oh, she had her reasons. "Higgins is such an ordinary last name," she always said when I complained. "I wanted something to jazz it up a little. Not Ann or Mary, they're too boring. You were born in Tallahassee, so I thought, why not?"

Then Liz would laugh and say, "Just be glad you weren't born in Peoria or Kalamazoo, kid."

Glancing at Dawn, I tossed some hair out of my eyes and said, "It's an old family name, but when I grow up I'm going to change it to something prettier. Like Tiffany or Meredith."

"I don't like my name either," Dawn said. "When I have a kid, I'm just going to call it honey or something and when it's old enough it can pick out its own name."

We paused by a water fountain and got drinks. Then Dawn asked me where I was from.

"Florida," I said. "I'm just visiting my uncle and aunt for a couple of weeks. Then I'm moving to California. My mother's on her way to Hollywood."

"Really?" Dawn looked impressed. "Is she an actress?"

That made me laugh. "Even though I have big teeth and a zillion freckles?"

I made Melanie nod her head. "That's just what they like in Maryland, I hear. Big teeth and freckles and red hair. And don't forget, you can tell jokes and walk on your hands and turn perfect cartwheels and draw almost anything. Not everybody is as talented as you are, Tallahassee Higgins."

"But they might think I talk funny. And suppose I don't know how to do their math and stuff?"

"Well, you just have to stay here for a little while," Melanie said. "Then you'll be in California where the sun always shines and the sky is always blue and the leaves never fall off the trees."

With that thought to comfort me, I fell asleep.

*

The next morning, after Uncle Dan left for the phone company, Aunt Thelma drove me to school. Normally, she told me, she would be at work before I left the house, but the bank had given her special permission to come in late today. She wanted to make sure I got to school on time.

"Now pay attention to where I'm going, so you'll know how to get home," Aunt Thelma said as she pulled out of the driveway. "It's only six blocks, and you'll probably meet some other children to walk with."

"Do any kids my age live near us?" I was watching a girl with long, brown hair walking along behind three younger boys, probably her little brothers. The boys were pushing and shoving each other, quarreling about something, and the girl was doing her best to ignore them. She stared at us as we drove past, and Aunt Thelma waved at her.

"That's Jane DeFlores and her brothers," she told me. "They live in the house behind us."

I turned and looked out the rear window at Jane and her brothers, still fighting, as they dwindled away in the distance. "Is she nice?"

Aunt Thelma nodded. "She's a lovely little girl."

Before I could ask her any more questions, we pulled up across the street from the Pinkney Magruder Elementary School. It looked like a jail. Dark-red brick, two stories high, little windows, and big, green doors at the top of a flight of cement steps.

Off to one side the playground swings blew in the wind, their chains making a sad, clanking sound. Kids ran around shouting and yelling. It made my stomach hurt just to think about meeting so many strangers.

"Did you know your mother went to school here?" Aunt Thelma asked. "And Dan and I, too." She smiled and smoothed her coat. "It seems like yesterday."

To me it seemed more like a hundred years ago. I simply couldn't imagine Aunt Thelma or Liz walking up these steps, going through the big, green double door into the dreary tile hall, breathing in the smells of spaghetti and hot dogs, floor wax and chalk dust. Frankly, it made me feel as if the building were full of ghosts.

In the office Aunt Thelma paused at a counter and waited for the secretary to look up from her typewriter.

"I was here last week registering my niece, Tallahassee Higgins." Aunt Thelma nudged me forward.

The secretary looked through a pile of papers on her desk. "Oh, yes, you're all taken care of, Tallahassee. You'll be in Mrs. Duffy's class — Six-B in Room 201. I'll buzz somebody to get you."

"Wait a minute, Tallahassee, I almost forgot." Aunt Thelma opened her purse and pulled out a key on a long chain, the kind you see most often attached to bathtub plugs. "Take this and don't lose it. I'll be home around four-thirty. You can have a couple of cookies and a glass of milk, but I expect you to clean up any mess you make."

Sticking the key in my pocket, I looked at the floor, too embarrassed to meet her eyes. Did she have to talk to me as if I were a baby while the secretary leaned over the counter listening to every word?

"Here's Dawn," the secretary said as a girl walked into the office carrying a hall pass. "This is Tallahassee Higgins, honey. Will you show her where Six-B is?"

Dawn's eyes slid over me, taking in my stiff, new jeans, my big teeth, and my shaggy hair, blown every which way by the wind. Wishing I'd brought a comb with me, I said good-bye to Aunt Thelma and followed Dawn out of the office.

Walking behind her, I noticed that her hair was layered in perfect waves, her jeans fit just right, and her pale blue sweater matched her running shoes. Dawn was the kind of girl everybody wants to sit next to, and

"Not yet," I said, "but her boyfriend knows a lot of people in the film industry, and he's sure she's going to be a big star."

Dawn sucked in her breath. "Aren't you excited?"

"Well, sure." I hesitated. What if I told Dawn that Liz was being considered for a role in a movie opposite somebody like Richard Gere? Would she believe me?

"Here's Six-B," Dawn said. "I'll save you a place at our lunch table, and you can tell me all about your mother. Okay?"

The minute we stepped through the door, everybody stopped talking and stared at me. A tall woman with gray hair got up from her desk and smiled at me.

"Welcome to Pinkney Magruder Elementary School, Tallahassee." Mrs. Duffy took my hand and squeezed it warmly. "We're so glad to have you," she said. Her voice was as soft and warm as her hands.

After introducing me to the class, she told me to take an empty seat by the window. "Your books are there already, just waiting for you. We're doing a review unit on fractions."

I sat down and stared at the initials carved into the top of my desk. If there was anything I hated more than math, I couldn't think what it was.

After a few minutes I glanced across the room at Dawn. She and a couple of other girls were passing notes back and forth. From the looks they sent my way, I was sure Dawn was telling them about my mother, the movie star.

I noticed Jane DeFlores, too, sitting a couple of rows away. She caught my eye and smiled, revealing a mouthful of metal braces.

"Tallahassee, do you know the answer?"

Startled, I stared at Mrs. Duffy and the problem she had written on the blackboard. It was long and horrible and full of weird symbols. The boy across the aisle waved his hand, bouncing up and down in his seat in his eagerness to be called on, and a girl poked me and whispered something about finding the common denominator, whatever that was.

My face reddening, I shook my head. "In my school in Florida, we hadn't gotten to fractions." Which wasn't exactly true. We'd gotten to them, but I hadn't paid any attention because I knew we were moving.

I expected Mrs. Duffy to frown or look cross, but she just smiled sympathetically and said we'd have to work on them after school or something. Temporarily relieved, I slumped farther down in my seat and hoped she wouldn't call on me again. Didn't she realize I was just visiting here?

After social studies and English, the bell rang for lunch, and Dawn and her friends, Terri and Karen, walked to the cafeteria with me. Although I could smell hot dogs and spaghetti and maybe a little sauerkraut, today's meal was pizza, green beans, bread, and cherry Jell-O.

As soon as we sat down, Dawn leaned toward me. "Do you have a picture of your mother?"

I handed her a picture Roger had taken last summer

at the beach. Liz was wearing a bikini, and her long hair blew in the breeze. I was standing next to her, squinting into the sun and hugging Roger's dog, Sandy.

"She's beautiful." Dawn showed the picture to Karen and Terri. "You don't look at all like her," she added.

"I take after my father." I slipped the picture back into my wallet and pretended I didn't hear Karen whisper, "Too bad."

"So is she really going to be a star?" Terri asked.

Before answering, I took a deep breath. "She might get a part in Richard Gere's new movie," I said. "He's seen her photograph, and he's really interested in her."

"Richard Gere?" Dawn choked on a mouthful of pizza. "Are you serious?"

I nodded. In my imagination I saw Liz in a studio, the lights shining on her golden hair as she and Richard played their parts. The scene was so real to me, I felt as if I were gazing into a crystal ball and truly seeing the future.

"The movie's called *The Island*," I began, "and it's about a beautiful woman who's on a honeymoon with her new husband, Richard Gere. She has a daughter by a previous marriage, but she leaves her with a cruel aunt while she goes off to the Caribbean."

As I talked, I could see the whole movie unfolding before my eyes: The daughter would be played by a girl even prettier than Dawn, but the aunt would look like the witch in *The Wizard of Oz*, and everyone in the audience would feel sorry for the girl.

"First you see how happy the mother is, laughing and

swimming and having a wonderful time, hardly ever thinking about her daughter," I continued. "And then you see how miserable the daughter is. She has to sleep in a cold room, and she can't watch TV or go to McDonald's or even drink coffee, all because the aunt hates the girl's mother so much."

"Get to the interesting part," Dawn interrupted, apparently not realizing that I was right in the middle of it. "Will your mother get to kiss Richard Gere?"

She and Terri and Karen all giggled and stared at me. "Sure she will," I said. "It's an R movie, you know." I poked my spoon into my Jell-O and it quivered all over as if it were alive.

By the time we went back to class, I had myself believing Liz was about to become the biggest star in America. While Mrs. Duffy droned on and on about U.S. history and other boring subjects, I daydreamed about my future in Hollywood. In my imagination Liz and I were walking along a beach. "I've missed you so much, Talley," Liz was saying as the Pacific Ocean washed gently over the sand and swirled around our ankles.

Then Richard Gere came along and offered to give me a part in the movie, too. "Talley's a wonderful actress," Liz told him. "She has this amazing natural talent. She might not be able to do fractions, but wait till you see her on the screen." Then she gave me a big hug, and I almost cried right there in school thinking about it.

Chapter 7

WHEN THE DISMISSAL BELL finally rang, I hurried out of the room. I didn't want Mrs. Duffy to catch me for a fraction lesson, and I didn't want to tell any more stories about Liz and her movie career.

As I crossed the street, though, I heard somebody call me. Looking over my shoulder, I saw Jane DeFlores, with her brothers at her heels, running to catch up with me. Although she hadn't sat with Dawn and her friends at the lunch table, I'd caught Jane staring at me several times.

"Mind if I walk with you?" she asked. I nodded while the boys stared at me as if I had just dropped down from another planet.

"My aunt says you live behind her and Uncle Dan," I said as we started up Oglethorpe Street.

"That's right." Jane turned to her brothers. "This is Matthew, Mark, and Luke," she told me. "If my mother has one more boy — which I hope she doesn't — she'll name him John. You know, after the fourth apostle."

The boys, who seemed to be about nine, eight, and seven years old, mumbled something, and Luke asked, "What are those brown things all over your face?"

Jane started to poke him, but I was used to people kidding me about my freckles. "They're spots," I told him. "I'm a leopard girl." I snarled and lunged at him, flexing my fingers like claws.

Luke backed away, but Matthew and Mark laughed. "They're freckles, dummy," Matthew said, and gave Luke a friendly little shove that sent him flying into a hedge.

"They go with her orange hair," Mark added. Then, to my relief, the three of them ran on ahead, giving Jane and me a chance to talk.

"Did you know that your mother and my mother used to know each other?" Jane asked.

"Really?" Liz had never mentioned any of her old friends to me. In fact, whenever I asked her about Hyattsdale, she always said it was ancient history.

"I heard my mother talking to your aunt on the phone before you came." Jane stopped on the corner. "Here's where I live. Would you like to come in and meet her?"

Although Jane's house had tan shingles and Uncle Dan's had gray shingles, they were exactly alike on the outside. Inside, though, they were very different. Some of the walls had been knocked out in Jane's house, making the rooms bigger and brighter, and a family room had been added onto the back; it had a slanted

46 ·

ceiling with a skylight and sliding glass doors leading out to a deck. Everything looked new and modern, especially the kitchen.

The boys had beaten us home. Matthew and Mark were playing a noisy video game, blowing up aliens and spaceships and shouting at each other. Luke was trying to get a Star Wars action figure away from a little girl — a sister, I guess — and a baby was crying in a playpen. It was like walking into a day-care center.

When Mrs. DeFlores saw Jane and me, she looked up from the onion she was chopping. I expected her to spread her arms and embrace me, the daughter of her long-lost friend. But even after Jane told her who I was, she just stood there, staring at me.

"So you're Tallahassee," she finally said. Looking at me hard from head to foot, she added, "You don't look a bit like your mother."

"That's what everybody says." I watched her chop the onion into smaller and smaller pieces. "Liz says I take after my father."

Mrs. DeFlores looked at me again and bit her lower lip. Without saying anything, she went on mincing the onion.

"Jane says you and Liz were friends," I went on, still hoping to get a nice response from her.

"We knew each other."

"But you told me you played together all the time," Jane said. "You made the path through the hedge running back and forth."

"That was ages ago, when we were kids." Finished

with the onion, Mrs. DeFlores dumped it into a bowl with some ground beef and turned her attention to a green pepper.

"Liz is on her way to California now," I said, taking a handful of cookies from the bag Jane held out.

"To be a movie star," Jane added.

"So your aunt told me." Mrs. DeFlores began mixing egg and bread crumbs into the stuff in the bowl. "Luke!" she yelled suddenly. "Leave Susan alone. If you hit her one more time, you'll be sorry!"

"But she has my Darth Vader!" Luke shrieked. "And she won't give him to me!"

"Give Luke his toy!" Mrs. DeFlores shouted. "Right this minute, young lady, or I start counting!"

Susan burst into tears and threw Darth at Luke. Grabbing his toy, he joined Mark and Matthew in front of the video game, and Susan followed him, still whining about something.

"As soon as Liz gets settled, I'm going out there, too." I raised my voice to get Mrs. DeFlores's attention. "I'll tell her I saw you."

Mrs. DeFlores nodded and packed the meat loaf into a baking dish. "Jane, don't eat any more cookies. You'll ruin your appetite for dinner."

As Jane started to lead me upstairs to her room, Mrs. DeFlores called after her, "Don't forget you have to set the table and do some other things for me in half an hour. You'd better not spend all your free time talking when I'm sure you've got homework to do."

"How many brothers and sisters do you have, anyway?" I asked Jane as she slammed her door to keep Susan from following us into the bedroom.

"Too many," Jane said. "Three brothers and two sisters."

"Janie, Janie, let me in!" Susan banged on the door.

"Go away, baby brat-face!" Jane opened the door a crack and yelled at Susan.

"Let me in." Susan tried to wedge her body into the room, like a door-to-door salesman.

"Mom!" Jane bellowed. "Make Susan leave us alone!"

To my relief Mrs. DeFlores called Susan and threatened to count again if she didn't come at once.

"Why'd you tell me our moms were friends?" I asked Jane as Susan stamped downstairs crying.

"I thought they were."

"Well, your mom sure didn't act like it." I went to the window and looked across the yard at the back of Uncle Dan's house. Frankly, I was very disappointed in Mrs. DeFlores but I didn't want to embarrass Jane by saying so. As soon as she'd told me her mother knew Liz, I was sure that Mrs. DeFlores would be crazy about me. Liz's friends always thought I was a scream.

But, as far as I could see, Mrs. DeFlores didn't like me any better than Aunt Thelma did, and I couldn't imagine her being friends with Liz. For one thing, she seemed years older. And she didn't have any sense of humor. Jane must have misunderstood her mother, I thought. Maybe she had been friends with Aunt Thelma, not Liz.

When Jane joined me at the window, I pointed at

Uncle Dan's house. "That's my bedroom window, right across from yours."

"Once I read a book about some kids who fixed up a tin-can telephone between their rooms," Jane said. "Maybe you and I could do that."

"Do you know how?"

"No, but my dad is real good at stuff like that. I bet he could rig one up."

While Jane and I were talking, I saw Aunt Thelma's car pull into the driveway. "I guess I better go." I picked up my jacket and started downstairs with Jane right behind me.

"You can cut right through our backyard," she said, "through the hole in the hedge. Come on, I'll show you."

"Where are you going, Jane?" Mrs. DeFlores asked. "It's time to set the table."

"I'll be right back." Jane dashed out the door before her mother could say anything else. "Want to walk to school with me tomorrow?" she asked as we paused by the hedge.

"Sure." I felt like laughing and jumping around and acting crazy; maybe Mrs. DeFlores didn't like me, but Jane did.

I watched her run back to her house, her long, straight hair flying out behind her. Then, pushing my way through the gap in the hedge, I blundered through the remains of a vegetable garden and hurried up the porch steps.

When I got inside, I saw Aunt Thelma standing in the hallway sorting the mail. "Where have you been?" she asked. "I expected you to be here when I got home."

"I was over at Jane's." I grabbed at the mail. "Is there a postcard for me?"

"It's a little early to expect one," Aunt Thelma said as I pawed through the fliers addressed to Occupant. "By the end of the week you should hear from your mother."

"It'll be sooner than that," I said confidently. "She promised she'd write every day."

Aunt Thelma went into the kitchen and got some things out of the refrigerator. "Here, Tallahassee, pare these for me." Handing me six potatoes, she began trimming the fat from a piece of meat while Fritzi snuffled around her feet, hoping she might drop something, I suppose.

"Was Liz ever friends with Mrs. DeFlores?" I asked Aunt Thelma.

"They knew each other." Aunt Thelma glanced at me. "Why?"

"Jane told me they were friends." I concentrated on scraping the eye out of a potato. "But Mrs. DeFlores acted like she didn't even want me in the house. Jane noticed, too, so I wasn't just imagining it."

"Oh, don't be silly, Tallahassee. Linda's very nice." Aunt Thelma put the meat into a frying pan without looking at me.

"Is that Mrs. DeFlores's name — Linda?"

Aunt Thelma nodded. "But she's Mrs. DeFlores to you."

"I always called Liz's friends by their first names."

"Maybe that's how they do it in Florida. Here that would be disrespectful."

"But were they friends?" I persisted. "She seems so much older than Liz, more your age."

Aunt Thelma glanced at me. "Not every thirty-year-old woman wants to look like a teenager."

I knew she was wrong about that, but instead of correcting her, I asked her if Liz and Mrs. DeFlores had had a fight or something.

"I told you, Tallahassee, I don't remember." Aunt Thelma turned away to fill a pot with water and set it on the stove. "Cut the potatoes in quarters and drop them in as soon as the water boils."

"But you must remember." I began hacking the potatoes. "It wasn't *that* long ago."

"Will you drop the subject, Tallahassee?" Aunt Thelma picked up a spoon and began stirring the meat in the frying pan, a frown sharpening the lines around her mouth. "Whatever happened between your mother and Linda DeFlores is their business, not yours."

Dumping the potatoes into the boiling water, I flounced out of the kitchen, getting the usual snarl from Fritzi. "You have bad breath," I whispered to him. "And you smell bad all over."

Chapter 8

J ANE AND I WALKED to school together every morning for the rest of the week. And every afternoon we walked home together. After I checked the mail, we usually went to Jane's house because Mrs. DeFlores wouldn't allow her to play at Uncle Dan's house unless Aunt Thelma was home.

Unfortunately, Mrs. DeFlores didn't act any friendlier. If she had been in a bad mood the first time I met her, I guess she never got out of it. At least not when I was around.

Sometimes Jane would try to get her mother to be nice. She would say things like, "Doesn't Tallahassee have more freckles than anybody you ever saw?" and Mrs. DeFlores would ask Jane when she was going to do her homework. Or Jane would hold up one of the pictures I'd drawn in art and say, "See what a wonderful artist Tallahassee is," and Mrs. DeFlores would say, "You're a very good artist yourself, Jane."

Finally Jane gave up and we would go straight to her room, avoiding Susan, and play Clue or Monopoly. If I forgot about the time, though, Mrs. DeFlores would shout up the steps, "Tallahassee, your aunt is home." That was her way of telling me to leave.

When I'd been in Hyattsdale for two weeks without a word from Liz, I started getting desperate. Where was she? Suppose she'd had an accident? Bob had taken me for a ride on his motorcycle once, and I hadn't been very impressed with his driving skills. For all I knew, Liz was lying dead in the desert or something.

Of course Aunt Thelma thought I was being silly. "The mail is slow, Tallahassee," she would say. "It takes a long time for a letter to get here from out west."

Uncle Dan was much more sympathetic. He gave me a big road map and helped me figure out which route Liz had probably taken. I cut out a little motorcycle I'd drawn with two people on it, making sure to include their helmets, and entertained myself by moving it along the red interstate highway lines.

"Oh, Bob," I would make Liz say, "When are we going to pass a post office? Poor Talley, I have all these postcards for her and I haven't got any stamps."

And the mother stealer would say, "Sorry, Liz. No time to stop now. We have to keep going till we get to Hollywood."

Vroom, vroom, vra vra vra-voooom! Away the motorcycle would go with Liz clinging to Bob and crying, "Please let me get some stamps, please, Bob, please!"

At night I talked to Melanie, and she always made me feel better. "Don't worry," she would say in her squeaky, little voice, "Liz will send you the ticket soon. Then you'll never have to see Aunt Thelma again."

*

One night, while we were sitting at the dinner table, Aunt Thelma gave me a hard time about moping. She said I should try thinking about somebody besides myself.

"After all," she said, "you have a roof over your head and three meals a day. That's more than some children have." Pointing her fork at my plate, she added, "Eat your spaghetti. You need to put some meat on those bones. Do you want to stay little and skinny all your life?"

I poked at the mess on my plate, trying to eat the meat sauce without touching the noodles. "I don't like spaghetti," I said.

Aunt Thelma frowned, but the phone rang before she could really get going on her favorite topic, the importance of cleaning your plate. "It's probably a salesman," she said as she went to the kitchen to answer it. "They always call at the most inconvenient times."

As I rearranged my spaghetti, I heard Aunt Thelma say, "Well, it's about time you called. Somebody has been very worried about you."

Leaping from my chair, I ran to the kitchen as Aunt Thelma said, "Yes, you can speak to her, but I want to talk to you before you hang up."

My heart was pumping so hard I thought I might die of cardiac arrest. "Liz, Liz!" I yelled into the phone.

"Talley, honey, how are you?" Liz sounded like she was calling from across the street.

"I'm fine, but why haven't you written to me? You promised you'd write every day!" I shouted.

"I'm sorry, Talley, but you know me. I kept meaning to write and then forgetting."

"Are you sending the ticket soon?"

"Oh, honey, things haven't worked out quite as well as Bob and I hoped they would. We don't even have a decent place to stay yet, just a room in a motel, sweetie."

She paused, probably to light a cigarette. "Bob found a job in some pokey little photography shop, and I'm waiting tables in the Big Carrot, but we're looking every day for something better so we can get you out here. We miss you so much, Talley, we really do, but we can't have you come right now."

"But what about the movies, Liz? What about those people Bob knows, the ones who were going to get you started?" I bit my lip and tried not to cry. What was she doing working in a restaurant? She didn't have to go all the way to California to be a waitress.

"It takes time, honey, to get into films, but I'm working on it. And Bob's friends are sure I'll make it. All I need is the right break."

"But can't I come out there now?" I clutched the phone and whispered into it. "I can't stand it here, Liz. Aunt Thelma hates me. She won't let me do anything.

I can't even stay up late and watch TV." I snuffled hard and tried to keep my voice low, but I knew it was rising up to a real mosquito whine.

"I don't care if it's just a motel, Liz," I babbled. "I'll sleep on the floor and I won't be any trouble at all. You won't even know I'm there. Just send me the ticket, please, Liz, please!"

"Tallahassee, will you calm down?" Liz sounded cross. "I can't handle all this emotion right now. I told you I can't have you with me yet, and you're just going to have to accept that."

"I don't think you even miss me!" I was angry now. "I'll bet you never think about me at all!" I yelled. "You probably go surfing and swimming and lie around on the beach all day while I freeze in Maryland. More than likely I'll come down with pneumonia and die and you won't even get here for my funeral!"

"Don't be silly, Talley! You're just a child and you have no idea what it's like to be an adult and have to earn a living and worry all the time about important things like buying food and paying the rent, which isn't cheap even in this crummy place. It isn't like I left you with strangers or something. You're with your uncle in the house I grew up in."

"You hated it here, and so do I! If you don't come get me soon, I'll do just what you did — I'll run away!"

"Don't you dare talk to me like that! You'll stay there in Hyattsdale till I send for you!"

"And when will that be?"

"Give me another month or two. That's not so long, Talley." Liz's voice softened a little and took on a pleading note.

"It's forever!" I looked up as Aunt Thelma appeared in the doorway.

"Let me speak to her when you're finished," she said.

"Aunt Thelma wants to talk to you," I said to Liz.

"Listen, sweetie, I can't stay on the phone any longer. This is really costing me. Tell her I really appreciate her taking care of you and give my love to Dan. Okay?"

Before I could say another word, the phone clicked, and Liz was gone.

As I started to slam the receiver down, Aunt Thelma grabbed it. "She didn't hang up, did she?" She spoke into the receiver, "Liz? Liz?" Then she turned to me. "Didn't you tell her I wanted to speak to her?"

"She said she couldn't afford to talk anymore," I yelled. Ducking under my aunt's arm, I ran out of the kitchen and up the stairs to my room.

"She isn't sending me a ticket," I cried to Melanie. "Not for a long, long time. And she's not a movie star yet. She's just a waitress like she was in Florida."

"Poor Tallahassee," Melanie whispered. "But don't worry. Maybe Richard Gere will come to the Big Carrot for lunch one day and he'll see Liz and decide she's exactly the person he's looking for. Then, before you know it, you and me will be in California lying on a beach with Liz and we'll all live happily ever after."

I hugged Melanie and thought about Richard Gere

walking into the Big Carrot. Liz would ask him if he wanted the special, and he would say, "I think I'll have you instead," and he would carry her out of the Big Carrot, just like he carried Debra Winger away at the end of *An Officer and a Gentleman*. "You're coming back to the studio with me," he would say, and overnight Liz would become a star and I would go to California.

Chapter 9

THE NEXT WEEK Dawn and her friends joined Jane and me at our lunch table. "I thought you'd be in California by now." Dawn took a sip of chocolate milk and stared at me.

"Well," I said, "they're having some trouble with the script. They're reshooting a lot of scenes, and they've put off going to the Caribbean. That's why Liz hasn't sent for me. Things are all up in the air right now. You know how it is in Hollywood."

"It's not easy to be a movie star," Jane added loyally. "I saw Meryl Streep once on *Good Morning, America*, and she said your personal life really suffers. You have to sacrifice an awful lot."

Dawn nodded. "Being a star must be worth it, though."

Terri agreed. "They have tons of money and big houses and fancy cars. They all drive Mercedes or Jaguars."

"So it's worth waiting for," Karen said, looking at me over her tuna sandwich. "If it's really true." She and Dawn exchanged a quick look.

"What do you mean?" I asked.

Karen leaned toward me, her sandwich forgotten. "Me and Dawn read lots of magazines, and we haven't seen anything about Richard Gere being in a movie called *The Island.*"

"That's because it's top secret, dummy." I glared at her, but I had this awful feeling that she and Dawn had decided that I was lying about Liz.

"You don't know anything about Hollywood, Karen," Jane said coolly, "so don't argue with somebody who does."

Karen picked up her tray. "I'm not sitting with anybody who calls me a dummy." She stood up, and Dawn and Terri followed her across the cafeteria.

Angrily, I watched them crowding in at another table. They were laughing now, and looking at Jane and me. "Stuck-up snobs," I muttered.

"Don't let them bother you," Jane said. "What do they know?"

*

To make things worse, I got in trouble with Mrs. Duffy that afternoon. She was already mad because I hadn't handed in my math homework. Then I got a bad grade on my spelling test, and I couldn't remember the year the Civil War began. She really blew up, though, when she caught me reading *National Velvet* during current events. She made me stand up and tell the whole class about it, and then she caught me as I was leaving and told me I'd better start putting more effort into my schoolwork.

"When you came to me," Mrs. Duffy said, "I didn't think you'd be here long enough for me to worry about your progress, but now you'd better start paying attention and stop daydreaming out the window. You don't want to repeat the sixth grade, do you?"

Well, of course I didn't. Nor did I want Mrs. Duffy to have the conference with my aunt and uncle that she was threatening. So I promised I would try harder.

"I hope so, Tallahassee." Mrs. Duffy smiled at me then. "You're a smart little girl. There's no reason for you to do so poorly."

She paused, and I started to stand up, thinking she was finished. Jane was outside waiting for me, and I didn't want her to freeze to death.

"Just a minute," Mrs. Duffy added. "Is there anything bothering you that you'd like to talk to me about?"

I rearranged my books to avoid looking at her. "No, ma'am," I said.

"I know you must miss your mother," the teacher said gently.

I fumbled with the zipper on my ski jacket, ashamed to tell her I was scared my mother had dumped me on Uncle Dan's doorstep like a cat she didn't want anymore. "She'll be sending me a ticket soon," I told Mrs. Duffy so she wouldn't feel sorry for me.

"I hear she has a role in a movie," Mrs. Duffy said. "You must be very proud of her."

I nodded without looking at her. "Can I go now?" I asked her. "Jane's waiting for me."

"Yes, of course, Tallahassee." Mrs. Duffy patted my shoulder. "No more reading in your lap, though," she reminded me. "And please hand in your homework on time."

"Yes, ma'am." I ran from the room and found Jane on the steps outside.

"Was she mad?" she asked.

I shook my head. "No, she just wants me to do my homework and stuff."

As we crossed the street, I asked Jane more about Meryl Streep. "Did she ever abandon her daughter or anything like that?"

The wind was whipping Jane's hair around her face, and her nose and cheeks were red. "I don't think Meryl Streep has a daughter," she said.

When I didn't say anything, Jane walked a little more slowly. "Are you worried about Liz?" she asked softly.

I shrugged and jammed my hands deeper in the pockets of my jacket. The wind was knifing right through my clothes and I felt like I'd never be warm again. Not even in the summer.

"Sometimes I think she doesn't miss me very much," I said without looking up from the cracked and uneven sidewalk.

"She's your mother, Talley. Of course she misses you!" Jane sounded shocked.

"Oh, Jane," I sighed. "You just don't know. Liz is so different from your mom." I glanced at her, wondering how I could ever explain Liz to a person who had lived in the same house all her life with both of her parents. She had brothers and sisters and grandmothers and grandfathers and uncles and aunts and dozens of cousins.

And Mrs. DeFlores stayed home all day and took care of her kids and cooked and cleaned and wore polyester slacks like Aunt Thelma and had her hair permed at a beauty parlor. She would never go around the block on a motorcycle, let alone all the way to California. She didn't want to be a movie star. Or a singer. As far as I could see, she just wanted to be an ordinary, everyday sort of person.

Grumpy as Mrs. DeFlores was, Jane was lucky in some ways, I thought. When she walked in her front door, she knew her mother would be in the kitchen, feeding the baby or fixing dinner.

"I think it would be wonderful to have a mother like Liz," Jane said, interrupting my thoughts. "A real live movie star. Just think, when she sends you that ticket, she may meet you at the airport with Richard Gere."

"By then, he might be an old man," I muttered.

"Don't be silly." Jane turned to me. "Do you know what my mother is doing right now?" Jane kicked a stone so hard it sailed up in the air and bounced down the sidewalk ahead of us, narrowly missing a skinny black cat.

"She's wallpapering the bathroom for at least the third time. That's *her* idea of fun and excitement. My dad says he's never sure he's in the right house because she's always redecorating and moving the furniture around."

"At least you know where she is, Jane." I bent down and called to the cat. "Here, kitty, kitty, kitty."

As he circled my legs, purring, I stroked him. He reminded me of my old cat, Bilbo, and I wondered sadly what had ever become of him. "I remember you," I thought, picturing his big, green eyes and his shiny, black fur, "even if nobody else does. And I miss you."

"When I grow up," Jane said loudly, "I'm going to have an exciting life like Liz. I'm not going to stay home all day and wallpaper bathrooms."

"Then don't have any kids, Jane." I watched the cat give himself a little shake and walk off, twitching his tail, his head high.

"Liz had you." Jane jumped up and grabbed a tree limb hanging over the sidewalk. She chinned herself and dropped back to earth.

"Lots of movie stars have kids," she continued, a little out of breath, "and they don't get married, just like Liz. And they still have exciting lives."

"You shouldn't believe everything you read in *People* magazine." I grabbed the limb and chinned myself five times in a row without letting my feet touch the sidewalk. I knew I was going to get mad at Jane if she didn't shut up about movie stars and their exciting lives.

"You sure are in a bad mood today," Jane said. "Just because of Dawn and Karen."

"Race you to Uncle Dan's." I started running before she had a chance to say yes or no. The big old houses on

Oglethorpe Street flashed past me, and I heard Jane yelling at me to slow down, but I couldn't stop. For a few seconds I felt as if I could run all the way to California without stopping once and get there before it was dark.

Chapter 10

ONE AFTERNOON JANE and I were slogging home under a dark sky. It was almost the end of March, but, except for a lonely crocus poking up here and there, it didn't look much like spring. The wind was still cold, the grass was brown and marshy with puddles, and the rain hung in huge drops on the bare branches and dripped slowly to the ground. A few drab little birds — sparrows, I guess — huddled together on the telephone lines, their feathers fluffed to keep warm. They made a sad, wheezing sound, nothing you could call a song.

"Want to come over for a while?" Jane asked when we got to her corner.

"Is your mother still mad about last Saturday?" I looked at Jane uneasily. Mrs. DeFlores had grounded Jane because we had gone to the park without telling her and come home with wet feet and muddy jeans.

"I don't think so." Jane didn't sound very positive, but she added, "We could go straight upstairs. I've got something to show you."

As soon as we were safely in her room, with the door shut, Jane pulled an old photo album out from under her bed. "I found this last night when I was looking for a dictionary. See if you can guess who the people are."

Opening the album, she spread it out on her lap. The first picture was of two little girls squinting into the sun. They were holding dolls, but their faces were too blurry to tell what they really looked like. Underneath, somebody had written, "Linda and Liz, Christmas, 1961."

"Is that my mother?" I stared at the little face, fascinated.

"Isn't she cute? Look at those long braids." Jane smiled at little Liz and then tapped her mother's face. "She's kind of pudgy, don't you think?" She puffed her own cheeks out and giggled.

Jane skimmed through the album, flipping past page after page of photographs of the DeFlores family at long ago Christmases, Easters, and Thanksgivings, every now and then finding Liz in one of them.

"Here she is when she was your age." Jane paused on the first good picture of Liz she'd produced. She was standing next to Mrs. DeFlores on the front steps of Jane's house, grinning at the camera, her head tilted to one side, her tawny hair hanging loose in long waves. She was wearing bell-bottom jeans and a tie-dyed T-shirt. Mrs. DeFlores, shorter and plumper than Liz, was dressed much the same.

"Don't they look funny? Like hippies or something."

Jane laughed. "I bet they thought they were so cool."

"I didn't reply. I was staring at Liz, wishing I looked like her. She didn't have rabbit teeth like mine, and she didn't have dirty-red hair. Even when she was twelve, Liz was beautiful.

Jane tugged at the page, trying to turn it. "Wait till you see the next ones," she said. "You'll die laughing."

Jane was right. When Liz and Mrs. DeFlores appeared again, they were teenagers. Right in front of our eyes we could see them changing. Liz stayed tall and skinny, but Mrs. DeFlores started getting a little plumper. Although she wore bell-bottoms, her hair wasn't nearly as long as Liz's, and she didn't wrap bandanas around it.

"Your mom was a real flower child, wasn't she?" Jane asked. "My father told me he used to tease her about being a hippie; he called her Hyattsdale's own Joan Baez because she used to play the guitar and sing folk songs."

"Who's this guy?" I pointed at a tall teenager with long, red hair. In most of the pictures, he had his arm around Mrs. DeFlores, but he often seemed to be smiling at Liz. "It's not your dad."

"No." Jane stared at the boy's face. "He must have been Mom's boyfriend." She sounded puzzled. "I always thought Daddy was her first boyfriend." She bent her head over the picture. "It's Liz he's looking at, isn't it? And she's looking at him, too."

I nodded and turned to the last page. There was only one photograph on it — a class picture, I guess — the kind you see in yearbooks. It was of the same red-haired guy, the one with the big teeth I'd seen in all the other snapshots. Across the bottom of it he'd written, "To Linda, with all my love, Johnny."

"Does he remind you of anybody?" I whispered.

Jane sucked in her breath. "He looks like you, Tallahassee!"

We stared at each other, then at Johnny. My heart was pounding so fast, I thought it would fly out of my mouth. If what I was thinking was true, it was no wonder that Mrs. DeFlores didn't like Liz or me.

"Can you find out anything about him? Like his last name or something?" I asked Jane.

In answer, she reached under her bed again and pulled out a Northeastern High School yearbook. Flipping to the seniors, she studied each face till we found him. "John Randolph Russell," Jane read, " 'Reds,' Gymkhana Club. Ambition: See the world."

Then we sat and stared at each other. "Liz never told you your father's name, did she?" Jane asked.

I stared at Johnny's dirty-red hair, at the freckles visible even in the photograph, at the big front teeth. "The only thing I really know about my father is that I look just like him."

We turned back to the album and studied all the pictures of Johnny. "What do you think happened to him?" Jane stared at me.

"I don't know, but I'm sure going to ask Liz." I gazed at Johnny's smiling face. He looked nice, I thought, and funny. In the old color prints, he was always clown-

"I'd be scared to," Jane said frankly. "She'd get really mad, I just know she would."

I stood up and started pulling on my jacket as Susan stuck her head in the door.

"You have to go home," she said in her usual bratty way. "My mommy said so."

I crossed my eyes at her and ran downstairs, passing Mrs. DeFlores in the kitchen. She didn't even bother to say good-bye.

*

At Uncle Dan's house I ran to the basket where Aunt Thelma always put the mail. As usual, there was nothing for me.

"It's about time you got home," Aunt Thelma greeted me. "Set the table and then help me fix the salad."

Wordlessly, I held out Johnny's picture. "Do you know him?"

Aunt Thelma snatched the picture out of my hand. "Where did you get this?"

"Never mind where I got it. Do you *know* him?" I reached for the picture, but she held on to it, scrutinizing it as if she was memorizing every detail.

"Of course I know him," she said slowly. "It's Johnny Russell. He lived right around the corner on Forty-first Avenue. I used to babysit for him."

"Does he still live there?"

"He was killed in Vietnam," she said softly, "just before the war ended."

I sucked in my breath and my knees felt weak. "He's dead?" I whispered.

ing around and making silly faces, standing on his hands sometimes or hanging upside down by his knees.

"Can I have this?" My hand hovered over the signed portrait.

Jane shook her head. "Mom would notice if you took that. Take one of the snapshots instead."

It was a hard choice, but I finally decided on a picture of Johnny sitting on a wall. He was wearing rainbow-striped suspenders, a T-shirt, and faded jeans. His feet were bare and his long hair was blowing in the breeze, and he was smiling as if the summer sun would never stop shining on him.

Just as I slipped the picture in my pocket, Mrs. DeFlores opened the door. I don't know what she was going to say, but when she saw the album and the yearbook, she snatched them away from Jane, her face reddening.

"What are you doing with these?" she asked.

"I was just showing Tallahassee some pictures of her mother," Jane said. "I didn't think you'd mind."

"Well, I do mind." Mrs. DeFlores glared at us, the books pressed to her bosom. She started to leave the room, then paused in the doorway. "Oh, I came up to tell you that your aunt's home, Tallahassee, so you can run along over there. Jane, you get started on your schoolwork."

We sat still for a minute, listening to Mrs. DeFlore go downstairs. "What do you think she'd say if yc asked her about Johnny?" I asked Jane.

She nodded, gazing past me as if she could see Johnny somewhere beyond me. "His name's on the Vietnam Memorial in Washington. Your uncle and I went down to see it."

"He's my father, isn't he?" My mouth felt funny saying the words — dry and stiff and sort of shaky — but I forced them out.

"Your father?" Laying the picture on the counter, Aunt Thelma opened a kitchen cabinet and started pulling out the things she needed for dinner. "Whatever gave you that idea?"

"Look at him." I picked up the picture and waved it at her. "He looks just like me. Same hair, same teeth, same freckles! He's my father, I know he is!" I was yelling now, and Fritzi was barking, circling my feet, making little dashes at my shoes and jeans.

"Don't shout at me like that!" Aunt Thelma slammed a can of paprika down on the counter beside the chicken she was preparing to cook.

"Then tell me the truth!" I wanted to throw myself at her, hit her, force her to be honest with me.

"The truth? You want the truth?" Aunt Thelma's face reddened. "I have no idea who your father is! I doubt your own mother knows!"

For a second everything in the kitchen seemed to freeze. Even Fritzi stopped barking as Aunt Thelma and I stared at each other. When she finally opened her mouth to say something, I ran out of the kitchen and up the steps to my room, clutching Johnny's picture in my hand.

Chapter 11

T HE NEXT MORNING while Jane and I were walking to school, I told her what Aunt Thelma had
said about Johnny dying in Vietnam. "She also said she
didn't know who my father was," I added, not men-
tioning what she'd said about Liz.

"Oh, Talley, that's so sad." Jane looked close to
tears. "He wanted to see the world."

"Well, I guess he saw some of it," I said, blinking
back my own tears, "but not a very good part."

We were passing Forty-first Avenue, and I paused for
a minute and looked at the big, old houses inching up
the hill toward the park. "Do you think his family still
lives there?" I asked Jane.

"Mrs. Russell," she said. "Why didn't I think of her?
"She must be Johnny's mother!"

Jane pointed up the street. "See that big house, the
one with the tower? She lives right there."

"Just Mrs. Russell? All by herself?"

"Mr. Russell died a long time ago," Jane said. "I never knew she had any children, but she has a big dog. You've probably seen her out walking him."

"She's pretty old, with gray hair and kind of strict looking? And the dog's black and white and about the size of a pony?"

Jane nodded. "That's her. Never talks to anybody, just walks along with her nose up in the air. She was my mom's English teacher, but she's retired now."

"But, Jane —" I grabbed her arm so tightly she winced. "If Johnny was my father, she's my grandmother! My *grandmother!*"

"My gosh, Mrs. Russell a grandmother." Jane shook her head. "She just doesn't seem the type."

"You better hurry up, Jane," Matthew yelled from almost a block away. "You're going to be late! You, too, Leopard Girl!"

"Come on, Talley." Jane started running. "If we're late one more time, Mrs. Duffy is going to give us detention!"

"Who cares?" I said, but I hurried to catch up with Jane. Any more trouble and Mrs. Duffy would call my aunt and uncle in for a conference. Aunt Thelma hated me enough already. For all I knew, she'd send me off to a foster home the next time I did something she didn't like.

*

That morning, instead of working on my report on Germany, I thought about Mrs. Russell and how I might introduce myself to her. As Jane said, she wasn't exactly a friendly person, certainly not the grandmotherly type. If the wolf had come to her house, I'll bet she would have run him off long before Little Red Riding Hood arrived.

I finally decided that I would walk up and down in front of Mrs. Russell's house till she noticed me. One good look and she would run down the sidewalk and throw her arms around me, sobbing with joy, delighted to find her long-lost, one and only grandchild.

Just as I was imagining this wonderful reunion scene, Mrs. Duffy announced that it was time for art, my favorite subject, the only thing I get A's in except P.E.

We lined up and went down the hall to the art room. Jane and I sat together, as usual. I was painting a picture of a girl surfboarding. The foam on the top of the wave looked perfect, but the girl herself wasn't quite right. Her head was a little too big for her body or something.

"Is that supposed to be you on your surfboard?"

I looked up, surprised to see Dawn standing next to me. She and Terri and Karen hadn't spoken to me for weeks. Once I'd seen a note Dawn had passed to Terri; in it, she'd said that I was stuck-up. "She thinks her mother is so great. Well, so what? She's still here, isn't she."

Dawn stared at the picture. I could feel her breath on my hand she was so close to it.

"No," I said, even though the girl had red hair and I'd been thinking about being in California while I drew. "She's just made-up."

"You're pretty good at making things up, aren't you?" Dawn looked me in the eye. We were almost nose to nose.

I noticed that Terri and Karen were standing behind Dawn. Terri had her hands behind her back, as if she was hiding something.

"Ask her," Terri prompted Dawn.

"How's that movie coming along?" Dawn pushed her hair back, showing off the little cloisonné earrings she was wearing.

"What movie?" I concentrated on the blue sky I was painting.

"You know. The one with your mother and Richard Gere." She popped her gum, and I could smell artificial grape. "*The Island* or whatever it's called."

"It's fine." I looked at her and frowned, stung into saying something. "Liz just called to say she's sending for me soon. They've definitely got a part for me."

"Really." Dawn looked at Terri and nodded.

"How about this then?" Terri waved the *People* magazine she'd hidden behind her back. Richard Gere grinned at me from the cover. "There's a whole article in here about him and this new movie he's making with Sissy Spacek. There's no mention of your mother or any film about an island!"

"You made it all up, didn't you!" Dawn popped her gum and smirked.

"Your mother isn't any movie star," Terri added, shoving her face so close to me I could smell her breath.

"Don't talk to me like that!" I put down my brush and clenched my fists. Boy, did I want to sock them.

Dawn leaned toward me, bumping the jar of water on the table. Before I could move my painting, muddy gray water ran across it, ruining the whole thing.

"Look what you did!" Without thinking, I picked up a jar of blue tempera paint and hurled it at Dawn.

As Dawn opened her mouth to scream at me, Mrs. Duffy appeared. "Tallahassee!" she said, staring at the jar of paint in my hand. "What's going on here?"

"Look at my blouse!" Dawn cried.

"She ruined my picture!" I held it up. The beautiful foam was running down the waves, the girl's red hair had spread all over the sky, and everything was streaked with gray.

"I didn't mean to!" Dawn glared at me. Blue paint dribbled down her nose and dripped onto her chin. It streaked her white blouse and tipped the ends of her hair. If I hadn't been so upset, I would have laughed.

Before Mrs. Duffy could say anything, Jane intervened. "Dawn and Terri started it! They called Talley a liar, and then Dawn spilled water all over Talley's painting."

"You shut up and stay out of this," Dawn said to Jane, her face red with anger.

"We didn't do anything, Mrs. Duffy." Terri looked very prim.

Dawn nodded. "Tallahassee threw the paint at me for no reason at all."

"You liar!" I was about to throw another jar of paint

when Mrs. Duffy grasped me by the shoulders and sat me down. "Get the table cleaned up, Tallahassee," she said. "And you'll have to see me after school."

"How about her?" I pointed at Dawn, but seeing the look on Mrs. Duffy's face, I went to the sink and got the sponge.

"Ooh, ooh, ooh," David Spinks giggled as I passed his desk. "You're in trouble now, Tallahassee Higgins!"

Jane picked up my picture. "Maybe after it dries, you can fix it," she said.

Yanking it away from her, I crumpled it up and tossed it into the trash can. "I never want to see it again," I muttered as I wiped the blue paint and water from the table.

*

When the three-thirty bell rang, Jane told me she'd wait outside on the steps, and Dawn tossed me a nasty sneer over her shoulder as she left the classroom. Reluctantly, I sat down in a chair beside Mrs. Duffy's desk and prepared myself for a long lecture.

"Well, Tallahassee," Mrs. Duffy began, "would you like to tell me why you threw the paint at Dawn?"

I shrugged and looked down at my ratty running shoes. "She ruined my picture," I mumbled.

"Surely it was an accident," Mrs. Duffy said quietly.

"It was the best picture I ever painted."

"That's no reason to throw a jar of paint in someone's face." She paused, waiting, I suppose, for me to say something. When I just sat there, staring at the hole in my shoe, she straightened a pile of papers on her desk.

"I think it's time I called your aunt and uncle in for a conference," Mrs. Duffy said.

I looked at her once, then returned to contemplating my shoes. I would have liked to have told her everything, but how could she understand about Liz? Or what it was like to wonder all your life who your father was and then find out he was dead.

Mrs. Duffy sighed. "Well, since you don't have anything to tell me, you might as well take out a piece of paper, and we'll review this week's math."

When I had finished doing twenty math problems, I ran outside and found Jane sitting on the steps waiting for me. We ran across the playground, racing each other to the swings.

I pumped hard, trying to get as far off the ground as I could, but I slowed down when I noticed that Jane had coasted to a stop. "What's the matter?" I asked her.

"Talley, is Liz really going to be in that movie?" The wind swirled Jane's hair in front of her eyes, and she tossed it back, frowning.

I scuffed my feet in the trough a hundred kids' shoes had scooped out under the swing. Without looking at Jane, I said, "What if she isn't? Would you stop being my friend?"

"I'll always be your friend, Talley, no matter what." Jane's swing creaked as she rocked back and forth. "I was just wondering, that's all."

"Well, she's not," I said, knowing I sounded grumpy and mad. "She isn't going to be in any movie, I don't think, and she doesn't know Richard Gere or anybody else. All she's doing is working in some restaurant called the Big Carrot." I started swinging really hard again so Jane wouldn't see me crying.

Jane didn't say anything, but she got her swing going too. Soon the two of us were flying back and forth, Jane up when I was down, me up when she was down. Then we started singing this dumb song we'd learned in music, "Little Red Caboose," until we were laughing too hard to pump our swings.

On the way home we walked up and down Forty-first Avenue so many times that I got a blister on my heel, but we didn't see Mrs. Russell. Not once did she come to the window to observe her own granddaughter wearing out her shoes in front of her house.

*

That night Aunt Thelma got two phone calls. The first one was from Mrs. Duffy, and Aunt Thelma was very angry when she hung up. She couldn't understand why I was doing so badly in school. "It's not as if you were stupid," she said. "You're lazy, that's what's wrong with you. Just like Liz, you think the world owes you a living."

Then the phone rang again, right in the middle of the scene we were having. This time it was Dawn's mother.

"You ruined a twenty-five-dollar blouse," Aunt Thelma said as she hung up, "and Mrs. Harper expects me to pay for it!"

"She wrecked the picture I was painting!"

"A picture?" Aunt Thelma stared at me. "You ruined

an expensive blouse because of a worthless picture?"

"It wasn't worthless! It was the best picture I ever painted!" Tears filled my eyes as I remembered the red-haired girl coasting down the perfect wave on her surfboard. "You know I get A's in art," I added, thinking of the value she placed on grades.

"Art and P.E.," she said scornfully. "The only subjects you're passing, and they're not even important."

"They are to me!" I glared at her and she glared back.

"You go to your room," Aunt Thelma said. "I've heard enough from you for one night!"

As I walked past the living room, Uncle Dan looked up. "What's the matter now?" He'd been so absorbed in the basketball game on TV that he'd missed the whole scene.

"Nothing," I muttered, "nothing at all, except I hate living here!" My voice rose, triggering another outburst of barking from Fritzi. "Shut up!" I yelled at the dog. "Just shut up!"

"Oh, Talley." Uncle Dan stood up and started toward me, but I ran upstairs to my room, leaving Fritzi barking at the bottom of the steps.

Hurling myself down on my bed, I pressed my face against Melanie. "We've got to get out of here," I told her. "Every day it gets worse and worse."

"You could run away," Melanie said. "Just like Liz."

"Maybe I will," I muttered. "They think I'm exactly like her, don't they? So maybe I should do just what she did. It would serve Aunt Thelma right."

Chapter 12

A COUPLE OF DAYS later Aunt Thelma, Uncle Dan, and I were sitting in my classroom. Mrs. Duffy began our conference by explaining that my math skills were at least two years behind my grade placement.

"What does that mean?" Aunt Thelma frowned at Mrs. Duffy.

"Well, it means that Tallahassee is working on a low fourth-grade level. She doesn't know her multiplication tables, she doesn't grasp the fundamentals of long division, and her fractions are very shaky. She should have mastered these skills before entering sixth grade."

Mrs. Duffy sounded apologetic, as if she herself had something to do with my inadequacies.

"It may be that the Florida schools have a different curriculum," she added uncertainly, rustling some papers on her desk.

"It's more likely," said Aunt Thelma, "that Tallahassee was never made to do her homework. You do realize that she has attended at least half a dozen elementary schools before coming here?"

Mrs. Duffy nodded. "I looked at her record." Smiling at me, she added, "Her language skills are excellent. She reads on a twelfth-grade level, and her book reports are a real treat. Very original and entertaining, and usually beautifully illustrated. She has a great deal of artistic talent."

Uncle Dan smiled. "She gets that from her mother. Liz could draw anything, especially horses."

"We're not here to talk about her mother," Aunt Thelma said. Turning back to Mrs. Duffy, she went on, "But you indicated there were problems with her language arts, too."

Mrs. Duffy nodded. "Tallahassee fails to hand in many of her assignments. And the ones she does give me are often incomplete or poorly done. Take her foreign-country report, fifty percent of her social studies grade this quarter."

I squirmed uncomfortably at the sight of the report she passed to Aunt Thelma. It was only a few paragraphs copied hastily out of an encyclopedia; my pencil had smudged, making my sloppy handwriting even harder to read. My map was half-finished.

The only good thing about it was the cover. I had drawn a little boy in lederhosen walking his German shepherd. It was definitely one of my best pictures, and I was proud of it. It wasn't enough to save my report, though, and I didn't blame Mrs. Duffy for giving me an F.

"When Tallahassee first came to Magruder, I thought she was going to be with us for a short time," Mrs. Duffy said to Aunt Thelma. "I didn't push her as hard as I should have. I realize that she misses her mother, but she'll have to work harder if she wants to go on to the seventh grade next year."

I lowered my head, feeling my cheeks turn red. My stomach knotted up and my mouth got dry. "I can do sixth grade all over again in California," I mumbled.

"Instead of falling back on that hope, Tallahassee," Aunt Thelma said, "I think we'd better see what you can do to improve."

"Yes," Uncle Dan agreed. "What can we do to help?"

Staring at the blocks of linoleum on the floor, I listened to them discuss setting up a contract. It sounded pretty awful — sitting down with either my aunt or uncle every night while they supervised my schoolwork — but to pass, I had to do it.

When we left the school, Aunt Thelma told me how embarrassing it was to hear so many awful things about me. "I simply do not understand you," she said. "Mrs. Duffy says you're smart, that you could do all the work easily if you'd put your mind to it. As far as I can see, you just don't care about anything!"

I played with the zipper on my sweatshirt, running it up and down the track. It was a beautiful day, and I wished I were in the park with Jane instead of trapped in Aunt Thelma's car.

"Now, Thelma." Uncle Dan looked at me in the rearview mirror and smiled. "You heard Talley. She signed the contract. She doesn't want to fail any more than we want her to."

Turning my head, I gazed out the window as the Hyattstown houses drifted sadly past, softened now by a mist of tiny, green buds. It was April. Where was Liz?

*

The next day was Saturday, and Jane and I went to the park. We were sure we'd see Mrs. Russell there with her dog.

"I'll go right up to her," I told Jane as we walked down Forty-first Avenue past Mrs. Russell's house, "and tell her who I am."

"Really?" Jane was impressed, I could tell. "Or you could ring her doorbell right now." She stopped, one hand on Mrs. Russell's gate.

I looked at the brick sidewalk marching straight across the lawn to the big, white house, at the neatly trimmed bushes flanking the front steps, at the door painted dark green, brass knob and knocker gleaming in the morning sunlight. Except for a few birds fluttering around a feeder hanging from a dogwood tree, nothing stirred.

"I don't think she's home," I said, hoping Jane wouldn't guess that I was scared to set foot beyond the wrought-iron gate.

"Her car's there." Jane pointed at a shiny Buick in the driveway.

"Yes, but she's probably at the park." I edged away up the hill, suddenly afraid that Mrs. Russell would notice me loitering in front of her house. Suppose she didn't recognize me?

The park was crowded with families. It was the first really nice day I had experienced in the state of Maryland, and I guess everybody was anxious to be outside. Jane and I walked around for a while, then we swung and played on the monkey bars.

While I was hanging upside down, Jane yelled, "There she is, Talley!"

I was so startled, I almost fell right off on my head, but I managed to twist around like a cat and save myself. "Where?"

"Right over there with her dog. See?" Jane pointed to the other side of the tot lot. Sure enough, there she was, looking the other way while her dog relieved himself on the grass.

"Come on." Jane jumped down from the monkey bars and ran toward Mrs. Russell. I followed her, my heart pumping, my mouth dry.

"What are you going to do?" I yelled at Jane, but she ignored me as she skidded to a stop in front of Mrs. Russell.

"Hi, Mrs. Russell." Jane smiled her best smile. "Have you met Tallahassee Higgins?"

Mrs. Russell shook her head. "I don't believe I have." She glanced at me with no more interest than a person might show in an ant crossing the sidewalk.

"You probably knew her mother," Jane said helpfully. "Liz Higgins."

"Liz Higgins?" My mother's name certainly got a reaction. First Mrs. Russell's eyes widened like a camera lens when there isn't much light, then they narrowed down again as her forehead creased. "I didn't know Liz had a child."

To my chagrin, Mrs. Russell did not embrace me. In fact, she did not even smile at me. If anything, she frowned.

"Talley's staying with her Uncle Dan," Jane went on despite the uncertainty creeping into her voice. "Liz is in California, trying to be a movie star."

"Is that right?" Mrs. Russell tugged her dog away from me. "Sit, Bo."

Bo sat, but he kept his tail going a mile a minute. His head tipped to one side, his tongue hung out, and he grinned at me. Unlike Fritzi, Bo liked me.

"You sure have a nice dog," I said, finding it a little hard to talk past the lump of disappointment in my throat. Why hadn't she noticed how much I looked like Johnny?

"Yes, he's very nice." Mrs. Russell smiled for the first time. "A little rambunctious sometimes, but he's only a year old. He'll settle down as he gets older."

"Does he like to chase sticks?" I was remembering Roger's dog and the great games we used to play on the beach. Bo reminded me a little bit of him.

"I'm sure he'd enjoy it if he had the chance." Mrs. Russell scratched Bo behind his ears. "But the leash laws are so strict in the park, I don't dare let him loose."

"Maybe I could come over to your house sometime and throw some sticks for him," I heard myself saying. "You have a real big yard."

Mrs. Russell looked at me hard then, and I smiled, hoping she'd notice my big old rabbit teeth. "I'm sure Bo would enjoy that," she said slowly. Twitching the dog's leash, she started walking toward the street. "Come on, Bo. Time to go home."

I trotted by her side. "Could I hold his leash for a little while? Me and Jane are going home, too."

She handed me the leash. "Don't let him pull ahead," she said. "I'm training him to heel."

We walked along silently for a while. A cool breeze tugged at our clothes and hair, making us all shiver a little. I guessed winter wasn't quite gone, but at least the birds were singing instead of wheezing and the leaves were getting bigger and greener.

"My mother says you used to be her English teacher," Jane said.

Mrs. Russell nodded. "I taught her and Liz and both your aunt and your uncle," she said, turning to me.

"I bet my mother was one of your worst students," I said, giving Bo's leash a little tug to remind him to heel.

Mrs. Russell made a funny sound, a sort of barking laugh. "Liz could have been my best student," she said. "But she was more interested in other things."

"Like what?" We were on dangerous ground, but I never have known when to keep my mouth shut.

She shook her head. "I know it must be ancient history to you girls, but I taught Liz in the seventies, and most of the kids were caught up in protest marches and demonstrations and all kinds of things. It was hard to convince them that Shakespeare was relevant."

"You mean Liz was against the war in Vietnam?" I'd seen pictures of antiwar demonstrations — kids waving signs and putting flowers in guns and things like that, but Liz had never said anything about being involved in demonstrations. For some reason, I'd never associated her with that kind of thing.

"Oh, yes," Mrs. Russell said. "Liz hated the war."

"Didn't you hate it too?"

"Of course I did." Mrs. Russell glanced at me. "Don't let Bo tug on the leash," she said gently.

"How about my mom?" Jane butted in. "Was she against the war?"

Mrs. Russell shook her head. "Linda wasn't the type to get involved in demonstrations. She was an honor student. Straight A's in everything."

Jane sighed. "She expects me to be just like her. Only she wants me to go to college."

"She should have gone to college herself." Mrs. Russell frowned again and quickened her pace. "Perhaps you'd better give me the leash now, Tallahassee. I have to stop at the post office before I go home."

I surrendered Bo reluctantly. "Can I come over next week after school and play with him?"

"If you want to." She waved to us and set off down Madison Street, walking briskly. Although she didn't look back, Bo did.

"Well," I said to Jane, "I guess she didn't realize that she was talking to her own granddaughter."

Jane shook her head and sighed. "She was friendly, though. And she did stare at you when I told her you were Liz's daughter."

"Maybe I should have walked on my hands or turned a couple of cartwheels."

Jane looked puzzled. "What good would that have done?"

"Don't you remember what it said in the yearbook? Johnny was in gymkhana, and in lots of pictures he's standing on his hands or doing something acrobatic." I turned a cartwheel. "See? I'm really good at gymnastics, too."

"What if you just asked her about him?"

"I was going to, but you changed the subject to your mother." I frowned at Jane, then pulled a flower off a forsythia bush hanging over the sidewalk. "Maybe when I go over to her house to play with Bo, I'll say something. When it's just the two of us. Her and me."

Chapter 13

WHEN JANE AND I were nearly home, she asked me if I wanted to eat dinner at her house. "Maybe your aunt would let you stay overnight," she said. "We could stay up late and watch *Creature Feature* on TV. Wouldn't that be great?"

"Would it be okay with your mom? I'm not exactly her favorite person, you know."

"You wait here, and I'll go ask her." Jane left me sitting on the deck's top step and ran inside.

Since it was a warm day, the sliding glass doors were open, and I could hear every word Jane said.

I could also hear Mrs. DeFlores. "No," she said.

"Why not?" Jane asked. "You're making spaghetti, so there's plenty of food."

"I said no."

"But I told her she could stay overnight and watch *Creature Feature* and everything!" Jane's voice rose a little.

"Do you know what 'no' means?" Mrs. DeFlores's voice was rising, too, and I hoped Jane would give up and come back outside. If she continued to argue with her mother, she'd end up grounded for the rest of the weekend.

"But you let Judy Atwood stay overnight!"

"That was different."

"What was different about it?"

"Judy Atwood is a nice girl."

If I'd had any sense, I'd have gotten up then and sneaked back to Uncle Dan's. But no, I had to sit there and listen to everything else Mrs. DeFlores had to say.

"Tallahassee Higgins has been a bad influence on you since the day she came here. She's as common as dirt and a liar and a troublemaker. I don't want her in my house!"

"Shut up!" Jane cried frantically. "She's sitting right outside!"

I heard a sharp crack and I winced, knowing Mrs. DeFlores had just whopped Jane.

"I don't care if she does hear me!" Mrs. DeFlores yelled. "Don't you ever tell me to shut up again!"

I glanced at the door, thinking I heard Jane coming, but Mrs. DeFlores stopped her. "You go up to your room right now, young lady, and don't you come down till I call you. And you can forget about Sunday. You'll stay here and help me clean house all day."

Afraid that Mrs. DeFlores was going to come outside and start yelling at me next, I jumped off the deck and

ran through the hedge. "Bye-bye, Leopard Girl!" I
heard Matthew yell from the house.

*

At the dinner table that night I could hardly eat anything. Just before we sat down, I'd tried to call Jane,
but her mother hadn't let me talk to her. "Jane can't
come to the phone," she said. "She's being punished."
Then she hung up. Just like that.

As I sat there poking my mashed potatoes, Uncle Dan
asked if I was feeling all right.

"I'm not hungry," I said.

"Eat your dinner before it gets cold," Aunt Thelma
said at once.

I shook my head and stared at the napkin in my lap.
I could hear Uncle Dan chewing, and the clock ticking,
and Fritzi clicking around in the kitchen. "I don't want
anything." I pushed my plate away.

"Maybe you should just go on up to bed then," Aunt
Thelma said. "That's where people who can't eat their
dinner belong."

"Fine." I carried my plate out to the kitchen, giving
Fritzi a wide berth, and went upstairs without saying
another word to either Aunt Thelma or Uncle Dan.

After an hour or two I heard somebody come up the
steps and knock on my door. Putting down *National
Velvet*, which I was reading for the second time, I told
Uncle Dan to come in.

He handed me a plate with an apple and a couple of
cookies on it. "I thought you might be feeling a little
hungry now," he said.

I shook my head, but I was glad when he sat down on the edge of my bed.

"Things aren't going too well for you, are they?" he asked softly.

I plucked at a tuft on my bedspread. "Mrs. DeFlores hates me," I told him. "She thinks I'm common as dirt and she doesn't want me to be Jane's friend."

Uncle Dan sighed and then cleared his throat. "Where do you get these ideas, Tallahassee?" he asked.

"I don't get them from anywhere." I glared at him. "I heard Mrs. DeFlores talking to Jane about me. It's a wonder you didn't hear her, too. She was yelling loud enough to tell the whole neighborhood!"

He lit a cigarette then, just like Liz would have. Exhaling the smoke slowly, he said, "It's your mom she's mad at, Talley, not you."

I stared at him, forcing myself to say it. "Liz stole her boyfriend away." I pulled Johnny's picture out from under my pillow. "Johnny Russell," I said. "He's my father, isn't he?"

Uncle Dan looked at the photograph and shook his head. "I don't know who your father was, Tallahassee. Liz never told me, and I never asked. I figured if she wanted me to know she'd tell me." He gave me a little hug. "But you do look a lot like Johnny. Both Thelma and I noticed it."

I stared at him, waiting for him to say more. "Did Liz like Johnny? Did they go out or anything?" I prompted him.

He sighed and took a drag on his cigarette. "Johnny

· 95

went with Linda all through high school," he said. "They broke up just before graduation, but only Liz can tell you what happened. Or Linda. It was all a long time ago, honey."

"Did Johnny go to Florida with Liz?"

"No. He got drafted. It almost killed Mrs. Russell. She was so against that war."

"Who did Liz run away with, then?" I hugged Melanie against my chest and watched Uncle Dan blow a perfect smoke ring.

"Oh, some draft dodger she met at one of those demonstrations," he said, as the smoke ring floated up to the ceiling and faded away. "She ran off with him without telling anybody she was leaving. Not even Johnny."

"I met Mrs. Russell today," I said. "I thought she might recognize me."

"Recognize you?" Uncle Dan looked puzzled.

"As her granddaughter." I began fiddling with Melanie's braids, trying to smooth them a little. "I'm sure I am," I added when Uncle Dan didn't say anything.

"You get the craziest ideas, I swear you do. You're worse than your mother."

I could tell by Uncle Dan's tone of voice that he wasn't criticizing me. There were things about Liz that he liked, even if nobody else did.

"Do you think I should ask Mrs. Russell about Johnny?" I asked.

"No." Uncle Dan sounded shocked. "She never has gotten over that boy's death. He was her only child."

"Don't you think she might like to have a grand-daughter?"

"Tallahassee, you stay out of that woman's business. Don't you dare say a word to her about this." He frowned at me. "I mean it."

Turning my head, I slid down under my covers. "If I can't have a father or a mother, can't I at least have a grandmother?"

"What?" Uncle Dan leaned toward me. "I can't hear you when you've got the blanket over your head."

"Nothing." I peeped out at him. "I want to go to sleep now, okay?"

"Sure, honey." He gave me a little kiss on the fore-head. "Don't let Mrs. DeFlores upset you, Tallahassee. I don't think much of a grown woman who takes out her anger on a kid. She's been married for years to a real nice guy. What's she still worrying about Liz and Johnny for?"

*

On Sunday I was bored without Jane to play with, so I went for a ride on Liz's old bicycle. It had been sitting in the basement with two flat tires for years, but Uncle Dan had painted it a shiny dark red and fixed it up like new. I'd never had a bike in Florida, and I loved cruising around Hyattsdale, seeing the same things Liz had seen when she was my age.

On the way home, I coasted down Forty-first Avenue,

past Mrs. Russell's house. When I saw her out in the yard digging in a garden, I slowed down and skidded to a stop, almost hitting her fence.

She looked up, startled by the screech of my brakes. "Well," she said, "good afternoon, Tallahassee."

Although Mrs. Russell didn't look particularly pleased to see me, Bo charged up to the fence, barking and wagging his tail at the same time. "Hi, boy!" I reached out and petted him.

While Mrs. Russell watched, Bo stood on his hind legs and licked my nose. "Can I play with him for a while?" I asked her.

"I suppose so," she said.

"Watch this," I told her and jumped over the fence the way I'd learned to go over the vaulting box in P.E.

"Next time, use the gate," she said, unimpressed. "You could hurt yourself doing that."

"Come on, Bo!" Picking up a stick Mrs. Russell had removed from the garden, I ran across the lawn and tossed it.

We played for a long time, and when Bo was too tired even to look at the stick, I showed Mrs. Russell my cartwheels.

"They're perfect," I told her, hardly out of breath. "Mr. Adams, my P.E. teacher says I have a real talent for gymnastics. Want to see me walk on my hands?"

She didn't say anything, so I staggered across the grass upside down, then showed her my walkovers and backbends. "I can even do the splits."

I grinned up at her from the grass, thinking she had to notice now. Hadn't Johnny been in gymkhana?

But all Mrs. Russell said was, "Your face is scarlet. Maybe you should rest for a while."

Disappointed, I watched her rake the soil in the garden. "Would you like me to help you with that? This guy Liz used to know had a garden, and I helped him with it a lot. We grew the biggest tomatoes you ever saw, but his dog kept eating them." I laughed, remembering how mad Roger used to get at poor old Sandy. "Did you ever hear of a dog liking tomatoes?"

"I'm about to quit for the day." Mrs. Russell looked at her watch. "Isn't your aunt going to wonder where you are?"

I shrugged. "She's probably hoping I got run over by a truck or something."

"Tallahassee, that's a terrible thing to say." Mrs. Russell leaned on the rake handle and stared at me.

"She doesn't like me very much. Nobody around here does, except Jane and Uncle Dan. But I don't care. Soon I'll be out in California with Liz."

Bo stuck his nose in my face then and licked my chin, and I started playing with him again.

"I think he's had enough excitement for one day, Tallahassee," Mrs. Russell said. "Come, Bo, time to get supper."

"Can I play with Bo again?" I followed Mrs. Russell halfway up the steps, hoping she might invite me inside.

"If you like." She paused on the back porch and

· 99

looked at me, taking in every detail, I thought. "You go on home now," she said.

After she closed the door, I turned and ran down the steps, vaulted the fence again, and pedaled back to Oglethorpe Street, wishing I'd had the nerve to say something about Johnny. I had wanted to ask her what he was like and how he died. Most of all, I had wanted to ask her if she was my grandmother. But all I had done was show off like a little kid.

Chapter 14

THAT WEEK I FINALLY got a postcard from Liz. It was pretty short:

Talley, honey — No money for a house yet, still working in the Big Carrot — Miss you heaps and hope to see you soon — Love ya! Liz

"So that's the way it is," Aunt Thelma muttered, reading over my shoulder. She shook her head and pruned up her face. "Well, it's what I expected."

"What do you mean by that?" I held my card flat against my chest so she couldn't see any more of it.

Aunt Thelma didn't say anything. Instead she picked up Fritzi and carried him away, calling him sweetums and dearest and asking him what he wanted for supper. I wouldn't have been surprised to hear him ask for Chateaubriand or steak tartare. If he had, I'm sure she would have given it to him.

I ran upstairs and shut myself in my room. "Look at this." I showed Melanie the glossy picture on the front of the postcard. "That's the Pacific Ocean," I told her. "See how blue the sky and the water are? The sun always shines in California, and it's never cold." I looked out the window at the gray sky and scudding clouds, at the trees tossing in the wind.

"But the back is the most important part." I turned the card over and showed Melanie the message. She stared at it, her expression never changing. "Liz doesn't say exactly when," I explained, "but we'll be together again soon, Melanie. Soon."

Lying down on my back, I gazed up at the ceiling, tracing patterns in the cracks and dreaming about California. If only Liz had been a little more definite. What did "soon" mean? A few days, a couple of weeks, a month? All of a sudden, I had an idea.

"You know what?" I grabbed Melanie and held her above me, shaking her a little for emphasis. "I'm going to call Liz up and find out what's going on."

"How can you do that?" I made Melanie sound wonder-struck. "You don't know her phone number, you don't even know where she lives!"

"But I know where she works! I can call Information in Los Angeles and get the number of the Big Carrot."

"Oh, Talley, you're so smart!" Melanie clapped her pudgy hands and smiled. "But what about Aunt Thelma? She won't let you make a long-distance call."

"I'll do it while she's at work." It was so simple, I couldn't believe I hadn't thought of it sooner.

*

The next afternoon, I persuaded Jane to come home with me after school.

"But I'm not supposed to go to people's houses unless their parents are home," she whispered nervously as I unlocked the front door.

"Your mother will never know. She'll think we're at the park." I led Jane back to the kitchen where Fritzi greeted us with his usual fusillade of barking.

To shut Fritzi up, I gave him a dog yummy. "Why can't you like me?" I asked him as he took his bribe under the table and started gnawing on it. His only reply was a low growl.

While Fritzi was occupied, Jane and I studied the phone book, trying to figure out exactly what we were supposed to do to call long-distance. After a couple of mistakes, I finally got the operator in Los Angeles and told her what I wanted.

"Which Big Carrot?" she asked.

"There's more than one?"

"It's a health-food chain. There must be more than half a dozen in Los Angeles."

"Well, can you give me the numbers of all the Big Carrots?"

Although she didn't sound happy to do it, the operator read off the numbers of eight Big Carrots, and I wrote them all down.

"Now." I looked at Jane, my hand poised over the phone. "Let's hope we find Liz before Aunt Thelma comes home."

"Are you going to ask her about Johnny?" Jane asked as I dialed the first number.

"Of course I am. Next to finding out when she's sending me my plane ticket, that's the most important thing."

While Jane hung over my shoulder, scarcely breathing, I called seven Big Carrots before I got the right one.

"Liz Higgins?" A woman's voice asked. "Yes, she works here. Do you want to speak to her?"

"Yes, please." Of course I wanted to speak to her — why else would I call?

"Hey, you seen Liz?" the voice yelled. "Tell her she's got a phone call."

Then, clunk, down went the receiver, leaving me standing in the kitchen with my heart going thump, thump, thump. Finally, somebody picked up the phone. "Hello?"

It was Liz, and for a minute I couldn't say anything. It was Liz, it was really Liz!

"Hey, is anybody there?"

"It's me," I whispered. "It's me, Liz."

"Who is this?" Liz shouted.

"It's Tallahassee!" I was so scared she was going to hang up that I yelled. "Your daughter, in case you forgot!"

"Talley, baby!" Liz sounded amazed. "How did you get my number?"

"From Information. When am I supposed to come out there, Liz?"

"Didn't you get my postcard?"

"Yes, but it didn't say anything. Please let me come out there, please!"

"Look, Tallahassee," Liz cut into my pleading, her voice sharp as a knife. "I've told you I can't afford it right now. It's just not possible."

"How about the bus? It's cheap." I was whining now, something I knew she hated, but I couldn't help it.

Liz paused to light a cigarette and then exhaled so sharply I could hear her. "You don't understand, Talley. Bob's friends turned out to be a bunch of losers. They don't know anybody. They just sit around all day drinking wine and talking about the good old days. And Bob is perfectly happy fooling around with them and riding around on his motorcycle. I swear I might as well have stayed in Florida."

"You mean you haven't met anybody in the movie business?"

"I'm sorry, baby. I wish I had better news for you." Then Liz started crying. "Look, honey, I can't talk now. I've got tables waiting, and I need all the tips I can get. Be good, will you? I'll call you, I promise."

Before I could say another word, she hung up.

I put the receiver down and turned to Jane. "Come on, let's go to the park before Aunt Thelma comes home."

Safely out of the house, Jane and I ran across the yard and down the street. When we got to the park, we collapsed on a bench, too out of breath to talk.

After a while Jane turned to me. "What did your mother say?"

"Not much." I sighed and watched a mother pushing a little kid in a swing. She was singing a song Liz used to sing to me about the big rock-candy mountain. "Things aren't as great in California as she thought they'd be."

Jane stared at me, her face solemn. "She hasn't met any stars or anything?"

I shook my head so hard my hair swung out and thwacked Jane's cheek. "And she's real depressed, I can tell, and I'm not there to cheer her up. Oh, Jane, she really needs me, I know she does."

Jane's hand closed over mine. "She'd send for you if she could. I'm sure she would."

Tipping my head back, I stared up at the sky. It was just starting to get dark. A star hung in the pale strip of sky above the treetops, and the air was getting colder. I saw the mother lift her little kid out of the swing and walk away, still singing.

"I guess we'd better go," I said to Jane. "If you're not home when the streetlights come on, your mother will ground you again."

Jane stood up, and we walked slowly out of the park. As we passed Mrs. Russell's house, Jane said, "Oh, Talley, you didn't ask Liz about Johnny."

"I didn't exactly have a chance." I paused by the fence. The kitchen light was on, and I could see Mrs. Russell sitting at her table eating dinner.

"It must be awfully lonely to eat by yourself every night," Jane said.

"You'd think she'd be glad to have a granddaughter, wouldn't you?" Happy scenes formed in my head like home movies as I imagined Mrs. Russell and me sitting around the kitchen table laughing and talking, Bo stretched out at our feet.

"The streetlights are on!" Jane gasped, scattering my daydream into fragments. "I have to go!" Leaving me behind, she ran for home.

Well, I didn't feel like running, so I dawdled along, looking in windows and imagining what the people inside the houses were like. Were they happy? Were they sad? Did they like living in Hyattsdale or did they all wish they were in California?

By the time I reached Oglethorpe Street, I was late for dinner. I got in trouble for that and for being out after dark. As a punishment, I had to spend an hour with Uncle Dan going over my math problems instead of watching even half an hour of television.

*

Two long weeks passed. Although no word came from Liz, Aunt Thelma's telephone bill arrived. I was in my room when she opened it, but from the way she called me to come downstairs, I knew I was in trouble.

She was standing at the foot of the steps with the envelope in her hand. "What is the meaning of this?" she yelled at me. "I've got twelve dollars and fifty-five cents worth of long-distance calls to California on my phone bill!"

"What are you talking about?" I stopped halfway

down the steps and stared at the bill she was waving at me.

"You made these calls, didn't you?"

"I just wanted to talk to my mother!"

"You told me you didn't have her number."

"I didn't! I called Information."

Aunt Thelma slammed the telephone bill down on the table. "First I had to pay for that blouse you ruined, and now this. I will not have you sneaking around behind my back, running up bills on my phone. Do you understand?"

As I started to run back upstairs, she stopped me. "What did Liz say when you talked to her?"

"She'll be sending for me real soon!" I yelled. "That ought to make you happy!" Then I turned my back and thundered up the steps.

Flopping down on my bed, I picked up Melanie and looked out the window at the gray clouds sailing across the sky. As I lay there, I saw a bunch of dead leaves spiral into the air, as if they were being sucked up by a giant vacuum cleaner.

"I wish I were Dorothy," I whispered to Melanie, "and a huge tornado would take me away from here. Maybe not all the way to Oz. Maybe just to California."

Chapter 15

THE NEXT DAY was Saturday. Jane was at the orthodontist, safely away from my influence, so I hopped on my bike and rode over to Mrs. Russell's. I wasn't ready to give up on her yet.

I found her in her backyard hanging a sheet on a clothesline stretched from the porch to the garage. Bo was frisking around, snapping at the towels blowing in the breeze.

"Do you want some help?" I vaulted over the fence again, leaving my bike locked to one of the palings.

Mrs. Russell mumbled something that sounded like yes through a mouthful of old-fashioned wooden clothespins.

"Don't you have a clothes dryer?" I grabbed one end of a wet sheet and struggled to pin it to the line.

Dumping the clothespins into a little bag hanging on the line, she said, "On nice days like this, I hang my sheets and towels outside. It makes them smell good."

She yanked a corner of a sheet away from Bo. "No, Bo! Bad dog!"

Bo immediately sat down and looked so ashamed of himself that I couldn't help laughing.

"Want me to take him for a walk?" I asked. "We could play in the park or something."

"I suppose that would be all right." Mrs. Russell looked from me to Bo and back. "But you'll have to keep him on his leash, Tallahassee. I've already gotten in trouble with the park police for letting him run free. Poor thing." She patted Bo. "You don't understand about leash laws, do you?"

When she went inside to get his leash, I followed her up the steps, hoping again to be invited in. "Wait here," she said to me. "I'll be right back."

I peered through the screen door at the big, sunny kitchen. Johnny's kitchen. One whole window was full of glass shelves, jammed with African violets, all blooming and healthy. They reminded me of Liz's futile attempts to grow plants; when they died, she said it was because she had a brown thumb, but I knew better. Plants have to be watered. You can't just go off and forget them if you want them to bloom.

When Mrs. Russell reappeared with the leash, Bo jumped around, his tail wagging. "He's so smart," she said. "The minute he sees this, he knows he's going for a walk."

She knelt beside him and clipped the leash to his collar. "Now you be careful with him, Tallahassee," she said. "And remember what I said about not letting him loose."

Mrs. Russell followed us down the sidewalk and waved as we started up Forty-first Avenue. "Be back in an hour," she called.

"Come on, Bo! Let's go, boy!" I started running as soon as we got to the park, and Bo lunged ahead like a racehorse, just flying along. I would have loved to unfasten his leash, but I was afraid Mrs. Russell would find out and never let me take him anywhere again.

We didn't slow down till we got to the pond. Then I let Bo wade into the water and drink his fill. I hoped Mrs. Russell wouldn't get mad when she saw how muddy he was.

On the way home, I stopped and let a bunch of little kids pet Bo. They all seemed to know him, and one of them wanted to know where Mrs. Russell was and who I was.

"She's at home doing the laundry," I said, "and I'm her granddaughter. That's why I get to take Bo for a walk."

"I have a grandmother," a little girl told me.

"Me too," another kid said. "Only she's out in Arizona. I'm going to see her this summer. On an airplane." He spread his arms like wings and ran back to the tot lot, making jet plane noises.

By the time Bo and I got back to Mrs. Russell's house, the leash hung slack between us. We were too tired to run.

"Did you have a good walk?" Mrs. Russell was standing at the gate waiting for us, her hands clasped in front of her, her back straight.

"Bo got kind of muddy," I said apologetically. "He waded in the pond and then he drank out of all the mud puddles we passed."

Mrs. Russell scratched Bo's ears. "This big oaf could find water in the middle of the Sahara Desert. Couldn't you, you silly old dog?"

Bo rolled over on his back and waved all four legs in the air while Mrs. Russell rubbed his tummy. "Who's the biggest rascal in the world?" she asked him.

Straightening up, Mrs. Russell smiled at me. "I imagine you're pretty thirsty yourself, unless you were tasting the puddles, too. Would you like to come in for a minute and have a cup of tea with me?"

I followed her around the house to the back door. Before she let me in, she made me wipe the mud off my shoes while she cleaned Bo's paws with an old rag. Inside, she sat me down at a big oak table, the kind with lion's feet carved on its legs, and poured tea into pretty little flowered cups.

"Cookies?" Mrs. Russell passed me a plate heaped high with gingersnaps.

While I was eating, Mrs. Russell said, "I was thinking about something while you and Bo were gone, Tallahassee. How would you like to give him a run every Saturday in the park? I could pay you a dollar an hour."

"Oh, you don't have to give me any money." I stared at her. "I'll do it for free. I just love Bo!" I bent down and ruffled his fur so she wouldn't see how excited I was. She must like me, I thought, she must!

"No, no, I insist on paying you, Tallahassee. That is, if it's all right with your aunt and uncle."

"They won't care."

She shook her head. "I'll call tonight and make sure it's agreeable to them." She sipped her tea. "I enjoy walking Bo, but I can't run him the way you can. He needs the exercise."

"Where did you get Bo?" I asked. "In a pet store or what?"

Mrs. Russell smiled at Bo. "One day last spring, I was out walking with a friend of mine. We'd taken a path that runs along the railroad tracks, and suddenly we saw a puppy sitting on the ties. If a train had come along, he would have been hit. We called to the puppy and he came right away." She paused and scratched Bo behind the ears.

"We couldn't leave him there," she went on. "Since my friend Emma lives in an apartment, she had no room for him, so I brought him home. I ran ads in the paper for a month, but nobody claimed him."

Bo made a funny little sound and put his paw in my lap, his head tilted, grinning at me. "Do you mean somebody just left him there? They abandoned him?"

"Maybe they couldn't keep him and they didn't know what to do." Mrs. Russell shook her head.

"They could have taken him to the pound," I said. "He would've been safe there." Bo scratched at my leg and whuffed gently. His eyes rolled sadly from my cookie to me and back again. "Can he have a cookie?"

"Just one. They're really not good for his teeth, but he loves sweet things." Mrs. Russell chuckled. "He's very spoiled, I'm afraid."

"How come you gave him such a funny name?" I watched Bo snap up the cookie. I think he swallowed it whole, it disappeared so fast.

"Since he was sitting on the Baltimore and Ohio railroad tracks, I called him Bo. You know, short for B and O."

"That reminds me of how I got my name. I was born in Tallahassee, Florida, so Liz did pretty much the same thing you did." I made a face. "It's not so bad naming a pet for the place you found him. Me, I would have preferred a real name."

"I wouldn't expect Liz to give her child an ordinary, everyday name," Mrs. Russell said.

I looked up, wondering if she was criticizing Liz. If she was, her face didn't give anything away. "Why do you say that?"

"Well, Liz never did things the way most people do."

I put my teacup down very carefully. It was so fragile you could almost see through it, and I thought a loud noise might shatter it. "Did you know my mother very well?" I asked cautiously, sensing how close we were coming to the question I really wanted to ask her.

"As I told you, I taught her." Mrs. Russell sipped her tea. "Then, of course, since she lived so close, I saw her around the neighborhood. Liz and Linda DeFlores and my son, Johnny, were all the same age, and they spent a lot of time together, especially when they were teenagers."

Mrs. Russell gazed past me toward the back door. "On days like this, they'd gather on the back porch. Liz would usually have her guitar and they'd sing. Poor Johnny — I could always pick out his voice. He was the flat one. But Liz — her voice was truly beautiful."

"I can't carry a tune," I told Mrs. Russell. "Liz says my father couldn't either. She says I look just like him, too." I leaned toward her, my heart pounding.

"What else did Liz tell you about your father?" Mrs. Russell was staring at me as if she'd never seen me before.

"Nothing. Except I have his hair and his teeth."

For a few moments neither of us spoke. Through the open window, I could hear a bird singing. Close by, someone started a power mower, and a car sped up the street.

Then the phone rang so loudly that I jumped. Mrs. Russell left the room to answer it, leaving me alone with Bo.

"Yes," I heard her say, "yes, she's here. I'll send her home right now. No, not at all, Thelma."

"Mrs. Russell came back into the kitchen. "That was your aunt, Tallahassee," she told me. "She wants you to come home for lunch."

"How did she know I was here?"

"Mrs. DeFlores saw your bike chained to my fence."

"Is Aunt Thelma mad?"

"I don't think so." Mrs. Russell watched me as I carried my fragile little cup to the sink and set it down carefully on the drainboard.

"That's a wonder. She's usually mad about everything."

Mrs. Russell rinsed the little cups and wiped them carefully. "Now, Tallahassee," she said gently, "you had better run along."

"It was Aunt Thelma's fault Liz ran away," I said as I edged toward the door, knowing I should leave but wanting to stay.

"That's really not fair," Mrs. Russell said. "People do what they want to do. Nobody makes them." She opened an old-fashioned kitchen cabinet and put the cups safely on a shelf.

"Sometimes I'd like to run away to California and find Liz," I said.

"Running away doesn't solve anything," Mrs. Russell said. "In fact, it usually gives you a whole set of new problems worse than the old ones. And it hurts the people you leave behind."

"It wouldn't hurt Aunt Thelma. She'd be glad."

Mrs. Russell shook her head. "What about your Uncle Dan? He's never gotten over Liz leaving. You wouldn't want to hurt him, would you?"

I turned my attention to patting Bo and tried not to think about what Mrs. Russell was saying. Of course I didn't want to hurt my uncle. I loved him. But Liz had loved him, too, and it hadn't stopped her.

"You really miss your mother, don't you?" Mrs.

Russell was standing beside me, so close I could have reached out and hugged her.

"Yes," I whispered, feeling a sharp-edged lump fill my throat. "And I'm so scared I'll never see her again. Sometimes I think she doesn't want me anymore." I cried then, letting my tears soak into Bo's fur.

Mrs. Russell touched my hair very gently. I felt her hand linger there, then slowly withdraw. "Don't cry, Tallahassee, don't. She'll come back. Give her a little time."

I wiped my eyes on my sleeve, embarrassed that I'd cried in front of Mrs. Russell. As I stood up, I looked into her eyes, wanting so badly for her to say the magic words, to tell me she knew who my father was, but she said nothing.

"Do you still want me to walk Bo on Saturdays?" I asked.

"Of course I do. I'll call your aunt tonight and tell her." She glanced at her watch and frowned. "Oh, dear, it's after one o'clock. Please apologize to Thelma for me. I'm afraid I've made you late for lunch."

After thanking Mrs. Russell for the cookies and tea, I waved good-bye and ran across the lawn to my bicycle. As I pedaled back to Oglethorpe Street, I thought about everything Mrs. Russell had said, especially about Johnny. I remembered the soft touch of her hand on my hair and the way she had smiled at me. Even if she never told me that I was her granddaughter, I was sure that I was. And I was also sure that she liked me. Otherwise, she never would have allowed me to walk Bo.

Chapter 16

A FEW DAYS LATER Jane and I came home from school and flopped down on Uncle Dan's front porch. It was a very warm day, too hot to go bike riding, too hot to walk to the park, too hot to do anything. Just to irritate us, Fritzi was standing on his hind legs peering through the window at us and barking. I had lived here now for nearly three months, and he still seemed to think I was public enemy number one.

"Poor thing, he wants to come outside," Jane said. "Would Fritzi baby stop barking if we play with you?" She pressed her face against the window and made little kisses against the glass.

"Are you nuts?" I stared at Jane, revolted at the baby talk she was cooing at my enemy. "Don't waste your breath on that monster."

"Oh, I love little dogs. They're so cute." Jane smiled

at Fritzi, who continued yapping and jumping up and down at the window.

"Yuck." In my opinion Fritzi wasn't even a dog. He was more like a stuffed sausage on four stubby legs.

"Do you have a doll?" Jane asked suddenly.

"I got one as a going-away present when I left Florida, but she's really ugly." I felt bad saying such a mean thing about poor Melanie, but I didn't want Jane to know that, next to her and Bo, my best friend was a doll.

"I don't *play* with her or anything," I added so Jane wouldn't get any funny ideas about Melanie and me. "Why? Do you want to have a dolly tea party or something?"

Jane shook her head and laughed. "I was just thinking of something we could do. I've got an old baby carriage at home. Suppose I get it and you get your doll's dress and we dress Fritzi up and push him around in the carriage."

"No way." I stared at Jane. "That's the dumbest thing I've ever heard of. Besides, Fritzi would bite your hand off if you tried to put a dress on him."

"Oh, come on, Talley. He'd look so adorable. I've got a little ruffly bonnet he could wear." Jane was poised on the bottom step, ready to run home and get the carriage.

Fritzi barked again, a long series of yaps. I looked at his pointed snout and mean little eyes and burst out laughing at the thought of him wearing a frilly bonnet. He would hate it, and it would serve him right for always being so nasty to me.

After telling Jane to get the carriage and the bonnet, I ran upstairs and picked up Melanie. "This is a terrible thing to do to you," I whispered, "and I apologize, but I have to borrow your dress."

Leaving her on the bed, I ran downstairs and let Jane in. Together we cornered Fritzi in the kitchen. By bribing him with puppy bones, we managed to get the dress and the bonnet on him. Although he snapped and growled, he didn't actually try to bite us, even when Jane sprayed him with some of Aunt Thelma's perfume and jammed him into the carriage.

"You hold him still, and I'll push," Jane said as she opened the back door.

We were halfway down the driveway when Fritzi jumped out of the carriage and ran like a mad dog across the lawn toward the street. He was slowed down considerably by Melanie's dress and the bonnet, which now covered his entire head, but Jane and I couldn't catch him.

I was laughing so hard I could hardly run, and Jane was pushing the doll carriage and shrieking, "My baby, my baby, save my baby!"

Too late, I saw the car coming down the street and Fritzi, blinded by the hat, running out in front of it. "No, Fritzi, no!" I screamed.

Shutting my eyes didn't keep me from hearing squealing brakes and then an awful thump. For a few seconds I stood still, trying to convince myself nothing had happened.

"Oh, no," Jane sobbed. "Oh, no, no, no." Her voice trailed away and I felt her hand close around my arm. "Is he dead?" she whispered.

Opening my eyes, I saw a woman bending over a small bundle of rags in the street. "Is this your dog?" she asked. Her voice was shaking and she looked very upset. "He ran right out in front of me, I couldn't stop."

Slowly, I walked toward her, not wanting to look at Fritzi, fearing what I might see. "Is he — ?" I whispered, unable to finish the question.

She shook her head. "He's badly hurt, though. Is your mother home?"

"No." I knelt down beside Fritzi. With trembling hands, I pulled the hat gently back. Fritzi's eyes were open, and he was staring at me. As I put my hand on his head, he whimpered.

"Here comes your aunt!" Jane gasped, and I froze beside Fritzi, watching the old Ford approach and brake to a stop.

The car door opened, and Aunt Thelma emerged. She stared at us for a moment, her face pale, her hands pressed to her mouth. "What happened?" she cried.

"Your dog — he ran in front of me," the woman began to explain, but Aunt Thelma dropped to her knees, pushing me aside.

"Fritzi!" she cried, "Fritzi!"

"It wasn't my fault," the woman said. "These girls had him dressed up in doll clothes. The hat was over his eyes, and he couldn't see a thing."

Ignoring the woman, Aunt Thelma turned to me. *"Tallahassee, what have you done?"* she screamed.

I backed away, terrified of the anger on her face. "I'm sorry," I said. "We were just playing with him. We didn't mean for him to get hurt."

"Would you like me to drive you to the vet?" the woman asked as Aunt Thelma lifted Fritzi and cradled him against her breast like a baby.

I watched Aunt Thelma get into the woman's car and then I ran after her. Pressing my face against the closed window, I cried, "I'm sorry! I'm sorry!"

Aunt Thelma glared at me through the glass. "You get in the house, Tallahassee Higgins! We'll talk about this when I come back!"

I stepped away from the car, and the woman drove off, leaving Jane and me in the street.

"I think I better go home, Tallahassee," Jane said uneasily.

"I told you it was a dumb idea, didn't I?"

"You don't have to yell at me!" Jane backed away, dragging the doll carriage with her.

"Well, you didn't have to bring that stupid carriage over here and spray perfume all over him!"

"I'm sorry!" Jane shouted. "I didn't know what would happen!" She turned and ran down the street, pushing the carriage ahead of her, and I went into the house, slamming the door behind me.

In my room the first thing I saw was poor Melanie, lying on the bed where I had dumped her, wearing her undies and her little shoes and socks and nothing else. Scooping her up, I fell down on the bed and cried till I fell asleep.

When I woke up, the room was dark and cold, and Uncle Dan was shaking me gently. "Tallahassee," he said, "how about changing into your nightie and getting into bed? It's almost ten o'clock, honey. You slept right through dinner."

"Where's Aunt Thelma?" I sat up, still clutching Melanie.

"She's asleep."

"And Fritzi?"

"He's going to be all right. Got his leg in a cast and a couple of cracked ribs." He patted my shoulder. "Don't you worry. That dog will be his old cantankerous self in no time."

"I didn't mean for him to get hurt, Uncle Dan."

"Oh, I know you didn't, Tallahassee." He gave me a hug. "Your aunt will calm down. Just give her a little time. That dog's like a child to her."

I smoothed Melanie's hair. "She'll never forgive me," I whispered. "I know she won't."

"What?" He bent his head closer to mine and I could smell cigarette smoke clinging to him.

Without thinking about it, I threw my arms around him and pressed my face against the scratchy wool of his shirt. "Oh, Uncle Dan, do you think Liz is ever going to send me that ticket?"

"Sure she will, Talley." He sighed and pulled away

from me. "Now you get ready for bed like a good girl, and don't you worry about Fritzi or Liz. Everything will be fine. You'll see."

He got up slowly and left me alone. Quickly, I pulled off my clothes, shivering in the cold, and got into bed. "Oh, Melanie," I whispered, "I know Aunt Thelma will hate me forever now."

"Maybe we should just leave for California," Melanie whispered. "Right this minute."

I shook my head and frowned at her smiling face. "You're so dumb, Melon Head. Don't you know you can't go anywhere without money?"

"Then get some," Melanie said. "Rob a bank or something."

"And besides I'm not exactly sure where Liz is."

"Go to every Big Carrot till you find the right one, dummy." Melanie smirked at me.

I hugged her and lay there for a while, thinking about Liz and how surprised she'd be if I showed up in California. She'd be working, I thought, waiting on tables, and she would come to my table. She wouldn't recognize me right away because my back would be turned.

"And what will you have?" she'd say. "The special is excellent today. Fresh cream of broccoli soup and tuna salad on a croissant."

Then I'd turn around and take off my sunglasses. Liz would gasp as I stood up and did one of my best soft-shoe routines for her, the one that always made her laugh. Grabbing my Glinda the Good Witch Magic

Wand, I'd tap her on the head and croon, "Be happy, Liz, be happy."

As I was drifting off to sleep, imagining Liz embracing me, tears of joy pouring down her cheeks, I heard voices from my aunt and uncle's room.

"Dan? Is that you?" Aunt Thelma asked. "I thought you were asleep."

"No, I was just checking on Tallahassee," Uncle Dan said.

"I hope she's satisfied now," Aunt Thelma said. "She's hated poor Fritzi ever since she stepped through our front door."

"Oh, Thelma," Uncle Dan began.

"Don't 'Oh, Thelma' me!" my aunt snapped. "You have a blind spot where that child's concerned. Just like with Liz, you think she can't do anything wrong. You saw where that faith got you with her mother!"

"Tallahassee feels awful about this, Thelma. She never meant to harm that dog. She and Jane were just playing with him, that's all."

"She's a cold, conniving little liar, just like her mother, and she knows you'll believe everything she tells you!"

"You don't mean that, Thelma." Uncle Dan sounded shocked.

"I mean every word of it! I knew I'd be sorry when I said she could stay with us! The sooner she leaves for California the better!"

"I've heard enough!" Uncle Dan's voice rose, too.

"Where are you going?" Aunt Thelma asked.

"Downstairs to sleep on the couch!" Uncle Dan shouted.

"Go ahead then!" Aunt Thelma said. "But don't come moaning to me about your back aching in the morning!"

Then the house got real quiet. I shut my eyes and tried hard to get back to Liz in the Big Carrot, but the things Aunt Thelma had said kept echoing in my head, driving everything else away.

Did she really think I was the kind of person who would be glad an animal was hurt? Even though I didn't like Fritzi, I felt terrible about the accident. All my life I would remember the way he'd run in front of the car and the terrible sound of the brakes. If I could make time go backwards, I would never take Fritzi outside wearing those doll clothes.

"Aunt Thelma's probably sorry the car didn't hit me," I told Melanie. "Only she would have wanted it to kill me, not just break my leg."

"What are you going to do?" Melanie wanted to know. "How can you keep on living with somebody who thinks you're an animal-hating, cold, conniving liar?"

"I'm going to have to run away," I whispered. "I can't stay here, I can't!"

Chapter 17

THE SOUND OF falling rain woke me up early the next morning. "Great," I said to Melanie. "A perfect day — dark and wet and horrible."

Swatting the button on my alarm clock, I lay on my back and listened to the water gurgling down the drainpipes. Closing my eyes, I let myself drift back to sleep.

"Didn't you set your alarm?" Aunt Thelma's voice woke me up. She was standing in the doorway, holding Fritzi. His leg had a cast on it, but otherwise he looked normal. In fact, he even growled at me.

Trying to overlook the nasty edge in her voice, I said, "I'm awfully sorry about Fritzi, Aunt Thelma. I didn't mean for him to get hurt."

"Sometimes sorry isn't enough." Her eyes were as cold as two pebbles on the bottom of a frozen stream.

"But I didn't think he'd jump out of the carriage and run into the street." I could hear my voice rising into a whine, and I tried to control it. "Jane and I were just playing a little game. We didn't mean —"

"I don't want to hear about it, Tallahassee." Icicles dripped from each word she spoke.

"You hate me, don't you?" I felt myself tightening up all over.

"Believe what you like," Aunt Thelma said. "I know you will anyway." Turning her back on me, she started to leave the room. "Get up," she said over her shoulder. "I have to go to work."

"You're a terrible person!" I shouted at her. "No wonder my mother ran away!"

"Don't you dare talk to me like that!" Aunt Thelma swung around, startling Fritzi. "I didn't ask you to come here, I didn't invite you, but while you're in my house, I expect you to keep a civil tongue in your head!"

"It's not your house! It's my grandparents' house, and if they could see how you're treating me, they'd hate you, too!" I cried. "You're the one who should leave! I wish Uncle Dan would divorce you!"

Before she could say anything else, I ran past her and locked myself in the bathroom.

"You come out of there!" Aunt Thelma shouted.

"Not till you leave!"

"Oh, have it your way! I can't be late for work because of you."

Clump, clump, clump, down the stairs she went. As soon as I heard the back door slam, I went into my room and got dressed. Jamming everything I owned into my backpack, I picked up Melanie and the picture of Johnny and ran out into the rainy morning. I knew it was too early to meet Jane, but that was fine. I was still mad at her, anyway.

By the time I got to Mrs. Russell's house, I was wet and cold. Pushing open her front gate, I ran up to the front door and knocked hard.

"Why, Tallahassee, is anything wrong?" Mrs. Russell stepped aside to let me come in.

Dropping my backpack onto the floor, I held out Johnny's picture. "I think you're my grandmother," I shouted, "and I've come to live with you!"

Mrs. Russell took the photograph and stared at me. Then she dropped to her knees and put her arms around me. She let me cry and cry without saying a word.

After I'd calmed down a little, she took me to the kitchen and fixed me a cup of tea. While I was drinking it, she sat quietly across from me. Finally she spoke.

"Would you like to tell me what's happened?" she asked softly.

Everything spilled out, not just Fritzi's accident and the horrible things I'd heard Aunt Thelma say, but also my troubles at school, my fears about Liz, and my hopes about Johnny.

"So I want to stay here with you till Liz sends for me," I said. "I'll be the best granddaughter in the world, honest I will. I'll help you and take care of Bo and do everything you ask me to. I'll even do my schoolwork," I added, thinking that was probably important to Mrs. Russell. "I won't be any trouble at all, I swear I won't!"

Again she was silent, too silent.

"You don't want me either, do you?" I leapt to my feet, knocking my fragile little cup to the floor. I saw it shatter into pieces like an eggshell as I grabbed my things and ran out the door.

"Tallahassee," I heard Mrs. Russell call, "Tallahassee!"

Ignoring her, I leapt the fence, almost slipping on the wet grass, and plunged through the rain back to Uncle Dan's house. Just as I rounded the corner, I saw Jane coming down the street, carrying her big, purple umbrella.

"Tallahassee, where have you been?" she asked. "I was just at your house, knocking and knocking."

I skidded to a stop and wiped the tears from my cheeks with my sleeve. "I went for a walk," I mumbled, too upset now to be mad at Jane.

"In the rain?" Jane stared at me. "And why do you have all that stuff?"

"Oh, Jane, I have to get away from here, I have to!"

"It's your aunt, isn't it? She must be so mad about Fritzi."

"She really hates me, Jane. And I went to Mrs. Russell and she doesn't want me either. I'm going to California to find Liz, then everything will be all right."

"But how are you going to get there?"

"Hitchhike. Walk. I don't know!"

"I have a lot of money in my piggy bank, Tallahassee," Jane said slowly. "Over fifty dollars. If I give you that, you could buy a bus ticket, I bet."

I sucked in my breath and clutched Melanie against my chest. I had never had a friend like Jane in my whole life. "I'll pay you back," I told her, "as soon as I can."

"Come on, we'll go back to my house and get it." Jane turned around and started running toward home.

"But we're supposed to be at school! What will your mother say?" I shouted as I splashed through the puddles behind her.

"I'll tell her I forgot my homework." Jane dashed up the sidewalk and let herself in the front door.

"Jane?" Mrs. DeFlores looked up from her sewing machine. "What are you doing back home?"

"Math homework!" Jane gasped. "Have to get it!"

Following her to her room, I shut the door behind me as Jane climbed up on her desk chair and took her piggy bank off the top shelf. He was silver and very round, and he had a big grin on his face.

"You won't have to break him, will you?" I asked as she set him down on her bed.

"No, he unscrews and comes apart." Jane opened her desk drawer and took out a little screwdriver. Inserting the blade in a tiny screw on the pig's belly, she opened the bank and dumped the contents on her bed.

Separating the paper money from the silver, we counted it out. Thirty-seven one-dollar bills, two fives, and five dollars and fifty-five cents in quarters, nickles, and dimes. "Fifty-two dollars and fifty-five cents," I said.

"That might be enough for two bus tickets," Jane said softly.

I shook my head. "No, Jane, you can't go."

"Why not?" She stuck out her lip and blinked hard as if she was trying not to cry.

"Because you *live* here. With your mother and father and your brothers and sisters. If you went, you'd be running away, which is against the law."

"But you said you were running away."

"Well, not really. I'm leaving here to go to my mother, who needs me very much whether she knows it or not."

Jane gnawed on one of her fingernails and stared at the picture of Holly Hobbie on her bedspread. "What do you mean she needs you?"

I sighed. "She just does. Liz isn't as grown-up as your mother, and she needs me to take care of her. Down in Florida, when she'd get depressed, I'd sing her songs and do dances like Fred Astaire to make her laugh. And I'd fix soup and tea for her, and after a while she'd feel better."

Jane started working on a new nail. "Once Matthew and me tried to do a tap dance when Mom and Dad were having a fight. We thought they'd laugh and forget to be mad, but they just told us to go outside so they could keep on yelling at each other."

I didn't know what to say. It had never occurred to me that Jane's parents fought. Of course, her mother was a grouch, but I figured poor Mr. DeFlores was used to that.

"Well, anyway," I told Jane, "I have to go out there and make sure Liz is okay. Then I'll tell her to invite you to come for a visit."

"Do you think she'll say yes?" Jane's eyes were shiny.

"I know she will. Especially after I tell her about the money you loaned me."

We sat on the bed silently, listening to the sound of the rain gurgling in the downspouts. Then Jane said, "I know you have to go, Talley, but I'll miss you so much."

"I'll miss you too, Jane, but I'll send you postcards whenever the bus stops." I took a deep breath. "You're the best friend I've ever had."

"You too, Talley."

Just then Mrs. DeFlores yelled up the steps. "It's almost nine o'clock, Jane! You better get to school!"

I stood up and stuffed the money in my jeans pocket. Then Jane and I ran downstairs and out the front door.

Chapter 18

"I HATE YOUR AUNT!" Jane said as we walked down Farragut Street toward Route One. "I hope she really feels bad about the way she's treated you."

"Are you kidding? She'll be glad I'm gone. But Uncle Dan won't be." I turned to Jane. "Will you tell him sometime how much I love him? I'll write to him from California and explain everything, but you tell him too, okay?"

"Sure," Jane said. "I like your uncle. He's nice. But I'm never going to speak to your aunt again as long as I live!"

"Me either!" We were at the corner of Route One, and I could see the bus stop about half a block away.

"Oh, Talley, are you sure you ought to go?" Two big tears welled up in Jane's eyes. "Don't forget me," she sobbed.

"I won't. Not ever." I hugged her, and then I pulled away from her and ran down the sidewalk toward the bus stop. I didn't look back. If I had, I might not have gotten on the bus lurching down Route One toward me.

"Do you go near the Greyhound station?" I asked the driver as the doors whooshed open for me.

"I sure do," he said. "I stop right across the street."

Dropping my fare into the box, I sat down on the seat behind him. "Will you tell me when we get there?"

He nodded and smiled at me over a wide shoulder. Then he eased the bus away from the curb. Glancing out the window, I saw Hyattsdale recede into the distance like a bad dream I hoped I'd never have again.

"Where are you going so bright and early on a school day?" the driver asked.

"To California to see my mother," I said, feeling important. I was the only person on the bus, and I wished the driver were my personal chauffeur and we could ride all the way to California together. Just him and me. The two of us, rolling on and on all the way across America, never stopping till we came to the Pacific Ocean, where Liz would be waiting for me.

"She wanted me to come ages ago, but my aunt and uncle wouldn't let me go. Finally, my mother sent me the money and told me to get the bus today," I told the driver, wanting the conversation to continue.

"Oh, yeah?" He braked sharply and shook his fist at a delivery truck that had stopped right in front of us.

Then, before I could tell him anything else, he stopped to pick up a couple of ladies.

"Charlie, how's it going?" The first one through the

door plopped herself down behind him, shoving me to the other end of the seat, and her friend squeezed in between her and me.

"Just great, Ellie," the driver said, and from then on, he forgot all about me. Those ladies talked his ear off about a friend of theirs who was just getting over some horrible operation. Maybe they couldn't read the sign over his head that said, "Please do not talk to the driver while the bus is in motion."

"Hey, kid," the driver said, suddenly remembering me. "This is where you get off." He pointed across the street. "That's the terminal, right there. You be careful now, don't talk to nobody. Lots of weirdos hanging out there, no place for a little girl like you."

"I'm not a little girl!" Glad I'd tucked Melanie out of sight, I hoisted my backpack onto my shoulder and walked past him.

"Just get your ticket, sit down on a bench next to some respectable person, and don't look at nobody, okay?" he continued.

"And don't go to the rest room unless you really have to, honey," one of the ladies added.

"I know how to take care of myself." I glared at them both. The bus doors closed and away they went, still talking. Probably about me, now that I wasn't there to hear them.

I could see right away what the driver meant about the weirdos. A ragged old woman was squatting by the terminal door. She had about five shopping bags gathered around her, and she was talking to her fist. She held it in front of her face and shouted at it. The fist nodded and jiggled back and forth, but it stayed right there, listening to every word.

I sidled around the woman, looking at her out of the corner of my eye till it hurt, but I don't think she even saw me. "You heard me!" she screamed at her fist. "That's right! That's what they want to do, but they can't fool me, no, not Tillie. They won't get away with it."

Inside it was almost as bad. The benches were full of people staring off into space like zombies, their suitcases and bags at their feet. All of them seemed to have horrible, hacking coughs, and I was afraid somebody would collapse and die right in front of me.

I found the ticket counter and took out my money. "How much does it cost to go to California?" I asked a woman who reminded me of Mrs. Duffy.

She started fooling around with the computer in front of her. "Are you under twelve?" she asked.

"I'm ten," I lied, remembering that Liz always said I was ten when we went to the movies. She didn't have to pay as much for my ticket that way. "My birthday is August fifteenth." I gave her a big grin so she'd think I was a nice little girl, not a liar or a cheat or anything.

She nodded. "Are you going with your family?"

"Just me. I'm meeting my mother." I grinned again even though she hadn't seemed to notice the first one.

"Um," she mumbled, barely glancing at me. Then she

started giving me all these options — family rates, specials, all sorts of stuff — but no matter how low she got, the fare was more than I could afford. Finally, I thanked her and told her I had to talk to my aunt about it.

I went around to the other side of the counter where the ticket agent couldn't see me and asked the lady at the information desk for a schedule of California buses. By studying it, I discovered I could get to Boulder, Colorado, for fifty dollars. Thinking I could hitchhike the rest of the way, I bought the ticket and sat down next to a nice-looking old lady. Taking Melanie out of my backpack, I smiled at her and she smiled at me. "So far so good," I whispered to her.

Since I had almost an hour to wait for the bus to Boulder, I pulled *National Velvet* out and started reading, but it was hard to concentrate. I kept expecting to see Uncle Dan come charging into the bus terminal with Aunt Thelma behind him.

Finally, the loudspeaker announced the arrival of the California bus and rattled off the places it was supposed to stop between here and there, including Boulder. Grabbing my backpack, I joined the group of people heading for Gate Twelve, handed the driver my ticket, and got on the bus.

I picked a seat way in the back, where I thought the driver might forget about me, and made myself comfortable. Maybe I could stay on this bus all the way to California if I hid in the bathroom or something. Let them do whatever they wanted when we reached Los Angeles — even put me in jail. I'd call Liz, and she'd take care of everything.

Rummaging in my backpack, I pulled Melanie out. "You look indecent," I whispered. "I'm embarrassed to be seen with you. Don't you have any clothes?"

I made her shake her head. "You let that dog ruin them, remember?"

Checking to see if anyone was looking at me, I held Melanie up to the window and watched Washington slide past. I was hoping to catch a glimpse of the White House or the Capitol, but all I saw were rainy streets jammed with cars and buses and block after block of row houses and little stores.

"Say good-bye to the nation's capital," I told Melanie. "We'll probably never see it again."

Stuffing her into my backpack, I slumped down in my seat and closed my eyes. How long would it be till I got to California? I wondered. The bus wheels rumbled *soon, soon, soon* till they put me to sleep.

I didn't wake up till the bus slowed down for its first stop in Hagerstown, Maryland. Waiting to get on were two people — an old man and a state trooper.

Chapter 19

W HEN THE TROOPER stopped to talk to the driver, I slid down in my seat and held *National Velvet* in front of my face. "Maybe he just wants a ride," I whispered to Melanie. "Or maybe he's after a dangerous drug smuggler who's riding this very bus."

But I heard the trooper walking down the aisle toward me, his shoes creaking with every step he took. I didn't look up and I didn't take down my book, not even when he stopped next to me and I could feel his eyes boring into me.

He cleared his throat. "Is your name Tallahassee Higgins?" he asked.

Without taking my eyes off the sentence I was reading over and over, I shook my head. "There must be some mistake. My name is Melanie," I mumbled. "Melanie Russell."

"Come on, Tallahassee." He took my arm and pulled me up and toward him. "Let's go," he said.

Everybody on the bus turned around and stared at me as the trooper led me up the aisle. I guess they all thought I was going to jail or something, and I was scared they might be right. Maybe that's what happened to runaways.

The trooper led me to his car and told me to get in the passenger side. Then he drove a couple of blocks to the state police headquarters. "Your aunt is coming to get you," he said. "She'll be here in about an hour. Have you had anything to eat?"

I shook my head. "I'm not hungry."

"How about a soda, then?" He paused in front of a vending machine and dropped in some coins.

Handing me the cold can, he took me into an office and gave me a long lecture about the dangers of running away. "Do you know how many kids disappear in this country every day?" he asked me. "How many run away and are never seen again?"

"I wasn't running away," I whispered. "I was going to see my mother in California."

"But you bought a ticket to Boulder. As far as your aunt knows, you don't have any friends or relatives there."

"I didn't have enough money to get all the way to California, so I was going to stay on the bus. I thought I could hide in the bathroom or something." I bit my lip to keep from crying and stared at a poster of missing kids hanging on the wall behind the trooper. Their smiling faces were all lined up under the words Have You Seen Me? I stared at each blurry face, hoping I might recognize one, but I was pretty sure I didn't know any of them.

"Are you listening to me?" The trooper stopped in the middle of his long speech about the terrible experiences of runaway kids. "What do you think would have happened to you in Boulder?"

"What difference would it make? Nobody would care." I could feel a big, hard lump filling my throat, cutting into it as if I'd swallowed glass.

"Do you really believe that?" The trooper leaned toward me, but I didn't look at him. The lump was making my eyes fill up with tears, and I didn't want him to see me cry.

"Why do you think I took you off the bus?" he asked.

I shrugged and tried to sniff back the tears. Thinking it might help to drink some soda, I took a swallow but it couldn't get past the lump, and I choked on it. While I was coughing, the trooper told me how Aunt Thelma had called the police and reported me missing.

"She was really upset when your school called to ask why you weren't in class," he said. "Believe me, Tallahassee, your aunt cares about you."

"Huh," I snuffled, still fighting the tears but beginning to lose the battle.

"And your mother — what about her? Don't you think she cares?"

That did it. Tears came splashing down my face, and my nose started running, and I put my head down on the desk and bawled like a baby. "I don't know if she does or not," I wept. "That's why I wanted to see her. To find out. And also to make sure she's all right. She doesn't know how to take care of herself very well."

He let me cry for a long time, and when I was done, he handed me a box of Kleenex. I used up at least a dozen blowing my nose and wiping my face.

"Now," he said, "I want you to promise me something, Tallahassee."

I looked at him then, and his face had a nice expression on it, kind of sympathetic and stern at the same time.

"I want you to promise me that you'll never try to run away again." He paused a moment, waiting for me to nod my head or something.

When I didn't say anything, he added, "You may not realize that running away is against the law. If you try it again, I'll see that you're put in a detention center for a while. I don't think you'd like it there."

"If my mother sends me the money, I can go to California, though." I stared at the missing kids again, and their faces made me sad. When those pictures had been taken, nobody had known they'd end up on posters and milk cartons and grocery bags all over America.

"If your mother sends you money, that's totally different." The trooper's words hung in the air just long enough to make it sound like a very big "if."

"And, in the meantime," he added, smiling at me, "you'll stay with your aunt and uncle the way your mother wants you to. Right?"

"I guess so," I mumbled.

"You don't want your picture on one of those posters, do you?" He had followed my eyes to the missing kids.

I shook my head and shifted my gaze to the linoleum floor. The poster was beginning to scare me; it made me think of dying and nuclear war and all the other frightening things that worried me sometimes at night.

Just then, the door opened and a woman stuck her head into the office. "Officer Milbourne, Mrs. Higgins is here for her niece."

Officer Milbourne stood up and held out his hand for me to shake. It was a big hand, warm and hard, and it squeezed my own very firmly. "She's probably going to be mad at first," he said, winking at me. "They always are when they're worried, but, remember, it's because she's upset. She wouldn't be upset if she didn't care about you."

I nodded, but my mouth felt dry and my stomach quivered. It was okay for him to stand there winking and grinning as if he were sharing a little joke with me. He wasn't going to have to ride all the way back to Hyattsdale with Aunt Thelma.

"Tallahassee!" Aunt Thelma rushed into the office. For a minute I thought she was going to throw her arms around me, but she stopped short a foot away from me and clutched her purse to her chest instead. "Thank goodness, you're all right!"

She was more than upset, I thought. She was mad, furious, ready to kill me. I wished I could stay here and talk to Officer Milbourne a little longer. Listening to him describe the horrible fate of runaways would be better than getting into the car with Aunt Thelma.

"You had your uncle and me worried to death!" Aunt Thelma frowned at me. "How could you do such a thing?"

I hoped Officer Milbourne would say that she should be glad that my picture wasn't going to be added to the missing-kids poster, but he had his head bent over a pile of papers on his desk.

"I just wanted to see Liz," I mumbled.

Aunt Thelma opened her mouth, then clamped it shut again as if she were forcing herself not to say something awful about my mother. "Can I take my niece home now?" she asked Officer Milbourne.

He came out from behind his desk, put his arm around my shoulders, and gave me a hug. "Tallahassee just misses her mom," he told Aunt Thelma. "Maybe you can help her get in touch with her."

I looked at Aunt Thelma hopefully, but all she said was, "Get your backpack, Tallahassee. It's time to go."

She thanked Officer Milbourne again for all the trouble he'd gone to, and then she herded me out the door and down the hall. The last I saw of Officer Milbourne, he was staring at the missing-kids poster.

*

Outside the rain had finally stopped and the sun had come out, heating up everything. The car was steamy and hot, and I got in reluctantly, knowing Aunt Thelma was getting ready to yell at me. For a few minutes, though, she sat absolutely still, holding the steering wheel so tightly that her knuckles turned white.

"Well," she said finally, "I have never been so mortified since your mother left! Of all the ungrateful, irresponsible, selfish things to do! Don't you ever think of anybody but yourself?"

I put my feet on the dashboard and started picking at the hole in my running shoe. I could feel a trickle of sweat running down my spine. "After what you said last night and this morning, I thought you'd be glad to get rid of me."

"What about Dan? Did you think about him, how he might feel?" Aunt Thelma struck the steering wheel with her fist. "You know how much Liz hurt him by running off. How could you go and do the same thing?"

"I'm just like her, aren't I? You've said it often enough!" My voice was rising, but I didn't care now.

"You think it's all my fault Liz ran away, don't you?" Aunt Thelma turned to me. "I tried my best to be nice to your mother, to understand, even to take the place of her mother, but nothing did any good. She was determined to go her own way, and she didn't care who she hurt. She never thought of anybody but herself!"

Aunt Thelma gripped the steering wheel and breathed deeply. "She took Johnny Russell away from Linda, then dropped him when somebody more interesting came along. What did she care about the people she left behind? She never gave any of them a second thought, not her best friend, not her boyfriend, not even her own brother."

I stared at my aunt, but she wasn't looking at me. She was scowling straight ahead at the parking lot.

"For eight months after Liz left, we had no idea where she was," Aunt Thelma went on. "Not a phone call, not a letter, not even a postcard. Dan thought she must be dead. Then she calls up and tells us she's had a baby and could he send her money to pay the hospital bills!"

Aunt Thelma shook her head. "And, of course, Dan did. He's been sending her money for years. I just hope she used it to take care of you."

I slid down in my seat to avoid looking at my aunt. "Of course she did, Liz always took care of me. I'm her daughter, aren't I?"

"Yes, and look at the way she's treated you. She's doing the same thing to you she did to Dan. Isn't that proof of what a selfish, irresponsible person she is?"

"She's my mother! I love her no matter what! And she loves me!" I shoved the door open and jumped out of the car. Without knowing where I was going, I started running across the parking lot.

"Come back here, Tallahassee!" Aunt Thelma yelled.

"Just leave me alone!" I cried. "I never want to see you again! Never!"

Glancing over my shoulder, I saw Aunt Thelma following me across the asphalt, running clumsily in her high-heeled sandals. Her face was red and angry, and her shoulder bag whacked against her hip.

"You stop right this minute," she shouted.

But I kept going. Like the gingerbread boy, I knew I could run faster than my aunt. When I reached the road, though, I looked back again. Aunt Thelma was still coming, her face redder than ever. Suddenly, her ankle turned under her, and she fell heavily to the ground. Her purse flew through the air, scattering its contents across the parking lot, but Aunt Thelma just knelt there on the asphalt, her head lowered. She didn't even try to stand up.

I watched her, waiting for her to do something. I wanted to run down the road toward the mountains and never look back, but I couldn't leave her all alone in the parking lot. Suppose she was about to have a heart attack or a stroke?

Reluctantly, I walked toward her, my feet dragging. By the time I reached her, she was sitting up, her face hidden in her hands. Her slacks were torn at the knee, and her arm was gashed above her elbow. Worst of all, she was crying.

Silently, I picked up her things — keys, makeup, pennies, breath mints, dog biscuits, a ballpoint pen from Suburban Bank, a couple of sticks of gum, some tissues — and put them back in her purse. "Here's your stuff," I mumbled. "Are you okay?"

She nodded and fumbled for a tissue to blow her nose, but she didn't get up. She just sat there and cried while I stood beside her, feeling the sun beating down on my head.

"I'm sorry, Tallahassee," Aunt Thelma finally said. "I shouldn't have said those things about Liz. I was just so worried about you, so scared, thinking I'd made you run off."

She squinted up at me. Her tears had streaked her cheeks with mascara, making her look like a sad clown.

If she had been Liz, I would have pulled my magic wand out of my backpack or told some corny jokes or done a little dance. Silly things always made Liz laugh. But Aunt Thelma and I didn't have any routines to help us when things went wrong. So I just stared across the parking lot at the mountains shimmering through a haze of heat and waited for Aunt Thelma to do something.

When she made an effort to get to her feet, I took her arm and helped her hobble back to the car. Without looking at me, she settled herself behind the wheel, started the engine, and drove slowly out of the parking lot.

Chapter 20

IN SILENCE WE drove down a highway lined with gas stations, shopping centers, and fast-food places. As we passed a McDonald's, Aunt Thelma made a sudden left turn into the parking lot. "Let's stop here for a minute," she said.

Inside, the cool air made me shiver after the heat of the car. Aunt Thelma got in line behind a couple of teenage girls. "It's dinnertime," she said to me. "Are you hungry?"

"Not very." Trying to work up an appetite, I read the familiar names on the big, yellow menu over the counter. Quarter Pounders, Big Macs, Chicken McNuggets, hamburgers, cheeseburgers — you could eat the same things in Florida, Maryland, California, and everywhere in between. At this very minute, for instance, Liz could be ordering a Big Mac and fries in Hollywood, and they would look, smell, and taste exactly the same as the ones I could order here. The only difference was that Liz would be eating them for lunch instead of dinner.

"How about a cheeseburger?" Aunt Thelma's voice

cut into my daydream. "I bet you haven't had anything to eat since breakfast."

The girl behind the cash register looked at us. "Can I help you?"

After ordering cheeseburgers, fries, and sodas, Aunt Thelma carried our tray to a shiny plastic booth by a window.

"Nice view," she said, pointing across the parking lot and highway to the mountains. "Some summers, Dan and I rent a cottage at Deep Creek Lake. It's a long way from here, but maybe this July we could drive up there. I'll bet you've never been to the mountains."

She sat down heavily and took a big sip of soda. The gash on her arm had stopped bleeding, but grits of dirt from the parking lot clung to it. "Here, Tallahassee." She shoved my cheeseburger toward me. "Eat up."

To avoid looking at the cut on Aunt Thelma's arm, I watched the people lined up at the counter and remembered the fun Liz and I used to have guessing what each person would order. "Here comes a Big Mac and a large fries," she would say when a fat lady approached the cashier. "And a small diet coke," I would add. Then we'd both laugh, especially if the lady really ordered what we predicted. It was funny how often we'd be right.

Stirring the ice in my cup with my straw, I wondered if Liz and I would ever sit around and laugh like that again.

"Tallahassee," Aunt Thelma said, "I think we need to talk about a few things."

I glanced at her nervously, then looked out the window, not sure what she was going to say next. Right under my nose, a car was backing out of a parking space. A man and woman were in the front seat, and three kids and a dog were in the back. They reminded me of the happy families you see in commercials. Blond, suntanned, laughing. Nobody sad or mad. Nobody fighting. They were probably going home to a nice little house with green shutters and a picket fence around it.

As they pulled out onto the highway, I wished all kids had the chance to live like that. No divorces, no fathers killed in Vietnam, no mothers running off to Hollywood. Couldn't the government pass some kind of a law to protect kids from bad things?

When the car was out of sight, I looked at Aunt Thelma. She was staring at me, waiting for me to speak. Had she said something I hadn't heard?

"Did you really think Dan and I didn't want you?" she asked.

"You said last night that the sooner I went to California, the happier you'd be." I poked at my cheeseburger, removing the pickle slice they always hid under the bun, but I still didn't feel like eating anything.

"I didn't mean that, Tallahassee," Aunt Thelma said. "I was so upset about Fritzi, I didn't know what I was saying."

"I didn't want him to get hurt, Aunt Thelma, really I didn't." Tears welled up in my eyes. "I'm so sorry, and I wish I'd never put him in that dumb doll carriage."

"I know, Tallahassee, I know," Aunt Thelma said softly. "I had a lot of time to think about it while I was driving up here, and I realize you and Jane didn't mean to harm him. It's just that he's an old dog, and I guess I expected you to treat him a little more kindly."

Her voice quavered a little, and I remembered what Uncle Dan had said about Fritzi being like a child to her. "I love animals," I told her, "especially dogs. And they usually love me, too. Mrs. Russell's dog is crazy about me, and so was Roger's dog. But Fritzi and me, we must have a personality clash or something."

Aunt Thelma sighed. "Well, he *is* a little grouchy sometimes. But he's not a bad dog, Tallahassee."

I wasn't sure that she was right about that, but I didn't feel like arguing with her. Instead I said, "I'm really sorry Fritzi got hurt, and I'll try to be nicer to him."

Slowly, out of the corner of my eye, I saw Aunt Thelma's hand advance across the table toward mine. When it was almost touching my fingers, it stopped. "Tallahassee, I know I haven't done all I could to make you feel welcome," she said. "I'm just not used to children. I don't know how to talk to them. And you and Dan seemed to be getting along so well, I thought I could just leave you to him."

"Uncle Dan is wonderful, and I didn't mean to hurt his feelings by running away," I said. "I love him. It's just that I love Liz more."

Aunt Thelma nodded. "Well, she *is* your mother." She touched my wrist lightly with one finger, then withdrew it to her side of the table with the speed of a sand crab darting back into its hole.

· 153

"I know you think I've been mean," Aunt Thelma went on. "But I didn't want you running wild the way Liz did." She paused and added softly, "Maybe I was too hard on you."

She gazed across the table at me. Her brow was wrinkled, and her hair was frizzy from the heat. Traces of mascara still clung to her cheeks. "I wish your mother and I had gotten along better," she said.

"If you'd just stop saying awful things about Liz —" I leaned toward her, wishing I could make her understand. "She's not like Mrs. DeFlores, but she's still a good mother. And she hasn't run off and left me, I know she hasn't! She loves me too much to do something like that to me."

"I'm sorry I said that," Aunt Thelma said. "I had no business talking that way."

She poked the last bite of her cheeseburger into her mouth and chewed it slowly. "Aren't you going to eat your sandwich?" she asked.

I looked at it and shook my head. "I can't."

For a minute I thought Aunt Thelma was going to get mad at me. She hates to see anything wasted, especially if she paid for it. But, instead, she turned her attention to the gash on her arm. "My goodness," she said, as if she was noticing it for the first time. "I'd better clean this up."

"Do you want me to help you?" I slid out of my seat as she headed for the ladies' room.

"You get the tray, Tallahassee. I can take care of myself."

I dumped our trash in the waste can. Then I grabbed a handful of paper napkins from a dispenser and followed my aunt to the rest room. I found her trying to clean her arm with wet toilet paper. "Here," I said, "I can reach that cut easier than you can."

I soaked the napkins, and she let me dab her arm gently, cleaning off the dirt and the blood. After rummaging about in her purse, she found a Band-Aid and let me stick it on.

As we left the ladies' room, Aunt Thelma looked at her watch. "It's after seven," she said. "We'd better go home. Dan must be worried to death."

*

That evening Uncle Dan and I sat down in a couple of metal lawn chairs on the front porch. All that was left of the day was a little band of pink just above the housetops, and the air was cool on my bare arms. Aunt Thelma was puttering around in the kitchen, listening to her favorite golden oldies radio station. We could hear her singing along with Julie Andrews. "The hills are alive," she warbled, "with the sound of music," and a mockingbird, hidden in the dark foliage of the cherry tree, joined her.

"Well, Tallahassee," Uncle Dan said finally, "your aunt tells me you had a good talk in Hagerstown. She's hoping things will be better now. What do you think?"

"She was nice," I said, "but I still kind of wish I could have gotten to California. I really miss Liz."

He coughed and took a drag on his cigarette. "It's not all that bad here, is it?"

I shifted in my chair, trying to find a more comfortable position, but the cold metal was unyielding. "Liz needs me," I told him. "I know she does."

"And you need her," he said softly.

"Officer Milbourne thought maybe you'd let me call her."

Uncle Dan coughed again and took a long drag on his cigarette before tossing it out across the yard. We both watched it sail into the darkness like a tiny shooting star.

"Well?" I leaned toward him. "Can I?"

When Uncle Dan busied himself lighting another cigarette, I felt my throat tighten up. "Is something wrong?" I clung to the armrests of the chair and tilted forward, staring at him.

"Tallahassee, honey, I tried to call her this afternoon. I thought she'd want to know you'd run away, especially if you were heading out to California."

"So what did she say? Is she mad at me?"

He shook his head. "She wasn't there, Talley. The girl on the phone said Liz left the Big Carrot a couple of days ago. She didn't tell anybody where she was going. She just didn't show up for work."

I stared at him, feeling my whole insides turn over. "They don't know where she is?"

"No."

"But suppose something happened to her?" I thought of the missing-kids poster. Did they have one for grown-ups too?

"Oh, I wouldn't worry about that," he said. "Believe

it or not, Talley, Liz can take care of herself. I expect she found a better job. We'll probably hear from her as soon as she gets settled."

He covered my hand with his. Like Officer Milbourne's, it was big and warm. "I didn't want to tell you," he said. "I knew you'd be upset."

Out in the kitchen Aunt Thelma was singing, "When the moon hits your eye like a big pizza pie," and I sat there, listening to her, trying to make sense out of what Uncle Dan had just said. If Liz didn't call me or write to me, how would I ever find her? Without wanting to, I remembered Roger taking Liz and me to the beach in his old truck. I always rode in the back with Sandy, and Liz and Roger sat up front, singing old Bob Dylan songs and laughing. Little did Roger know then that Liz would just pack up and move someday without even telling him good-bye. Had she done the same thing to me that she'd done to Roger and Johnny and Uncle Dan?

Without saying anything, I jumped out of my chair, letting it crash to the floor behind me as I ran into the house. I didn't even answer Uncle Dan when he called out to me. I went straight upstairs to my room and slammed the door shut.

Alone in the darkness, I saw Liz's horses flutter in the draft the door had made. "What kind of a mother are you?" I shouted at the pictures. "How could you do this to me?"

Furiously, I yanked the horses off the wall, tearing them to pieces, stamping them under my feet till there was nothing left of them but little shreds of crumpled paper.

When the walls were bare, I grabbed Melanie out of my backpack and flopped down on my bed. I was so mad I wasn't even crying. "I hate Liz," I whispered to Melanie. "I hate her, and I never want to see her again!"

Chapter 21

THE NEXT MORNING Aunt Thelma woke me up. "Time to get ready for school," she said, as if nothing had happened. "I let you sleep late, so I have to leave for work now." She smiled a little nervously. "When you come home from school, be sure and check the Crockpot. I've got spaghetti sauce in it, and it ought to be stirred."

I lay in bed for a minute looking at the squares of dark wallpaper where Liz's horses used to hang. Aunt Thelma hadn't seemed to notice them or the torn paper littering the floor. As her car backed out of the driveway, I sat up and stretched. "Well, Melanie," I said, "it's back to good old Pinkney Magruder after all. I guess we'll never see California now."

Poor, dressless Melanie, wearing only panties, socks, and shoes, smiled bravely. "I was kind of scared on that big bus, anyway," she said.

Giving her a hug, I went downstairs and fixed my

breakfast. Before I'd finished eating my cereal, Janc was knocking at the back door.

"Talley," she cried, "my mother told me what happened!"

I stared at Jane, my spoon halfway to my mouth. "How did *she* know?"

"Before she called the police, your aunt called my mom to see if you were at our house." Jane sat down across from me and picked up half a piece of toast. "Can I have this?"

I nodded and she gobbled it up, strawberry jam and all. "I'm glad you're back," she said, her mouth full, "because I would have missed you a whole lot, but I'm sorry you didn't get to see your mom. I was thinking of you riding the waves on your surfboard and walking along the beach with Liz, maybe doing one of your tap-dance routines."

I poked at my cereal, soggy and bland, drowned in milk. "It wouldn't have been like that, Jane," I said. "It wouldn't have been like that at all."

"What do you mean?" Jane licked jam from one of her fingers and stared at me, puzzled.

"Liz wouldn't have been there," I told her. "She quit her job at the Big Carrot, and nobody even knows where she is."

Jane sucked in her breath. "Are you going to call the police and report her as a missing person?"

I shook my head. "Uncle Dan says she probably found a better job. He thinks she'll call and tell us about it." I dumped what was left of my cereal into the garbage disposal.

"You know what?" I glared at Jane. "I don't even care anymore! I'm beginning to think Aunt Thelma is right about her. Look at the way she treated Johnny and Roger. And now me, her own daughter!"

"Oh, Talley." Jane cupped her chin in her hands and said nothing while I gave Fritzi a puppy bone and patted his hard little head. She looked so sad, you'd have thought her mother was missing, too.

"We'd better go," I said. "It's ten of nine."

On the way to school I told Jane the Greyhound bus company was going to send us a refund, but even the prospect of getting her money back didn't cheer her up. She plodded silently beside me, her head down, kicking at stones.

When we reached the edge of the playground, though, Jane turned to me, smiling. "I figured it all out," she said. "Liz is coming to get you! She wants to surprise you!"

I stared at Jane, astonished. I hadn't even thought of that. "Do you really think so?"

"Of course! Maybe she'll be waiting for you when you get home from school this very afternoon!" Jane clapped her hands and laughed. "Oh, Talley, wouldn't that be neat?"

All day in school I thought about Jane's theory. Mrs. Duffy had to call on me twice in math to get my attention, and even then I didn't know the answer. When the dismissal bell rang, I still hadn't convinced myself that Liz was on her way back to Maryland. No matter what Jane thought, I had a feeling that Liz was gone forever.

*

On Saturday Jane had her usual date with the orthodontist. Even though I wasn't sure Mrs. Russell would want to see me again, I rode my bicycle up Forty-first Avenue, hoping Bo would be in the yard. He still liked me, I was sure of that.

As I pedaled past her house, I saw Mrs. Russell tending her garden. She was wearing a round, straw hat and an apron over her dress. In her hand was a big tin watering can like Farmer McGregor's.

Although she didn't see me, Bo did. He ran to the fence, barking and wagging his tail, and I stopped to pet him. While I had my head bent over his, I saw Mrs. Russell's tennis shoes striding across the grass toward me.

"Are you here to walk Bo, Tallahassee?" she asked.

Without looking up from Bo, I nodded. "If you still want me to."

"Why wouldn't I want you to?"

Her voice was no cooler than usual, so I glanced up at her. She was just standing there, a trowel in one hand, the watering can in the other, staring down at me. A tiny frown creased her forehead.

"I thought you might be mad at me." I returned my attention to Bo, who was trying to lick my nose.

"Because of last week?" Mrs. Russell touched my hair lightly. "I think I'm the one who owes you an apology, Tallahassee, but we'll talk more about that later. First take Bo for his walk. He needs a good run, dear."

I jumped the fence and followed her toward the house, my heart thumping. I was so happy, I felt like turning cartwheels across the lawn. She wasn't mad at me, she wasn't mad!

Snapping the leash to Bo's collar, I led him down the walk and up the hill to the park. We had a wonderful time, but I brought him home even muddier than he'd been last Saturday. He was so dirty, Mrs. Russell and I had to hose his legs and paws before he could go inside.

"We'll have lemonade on the screened porch," Mrs. Russell said, leading me through a side door. We seated ourselves at a little table covered with a checked cloth, and she poured us each a tall glass of lemonade from a pitcher.

After passing me a plate heaped with chocolate chip cookies, Mrs. Russell opened a photo album and showed me a picture of a boy with red hair, freckles, and big teeth.

"I've been doing a lot of thinking, Tallahassee," she said. "This is Johnny when he was your age. As you can see, you look very much like him." She paused briefly. "That could be merely a coincidence, of course. But I think, considering the facts as we know them, he might very well have been your father."

I looked at Mrs. Russell, scarcely daring to breathe.

"Then you would be my grandmother," I whispered.

She smiled and nodded. "But we'll never know for sure. Unless Liz tells us."

She sipped her lemonade. "You see, I didn't know Liz had a child. You came as a complete surprise to me." She gazed past me at the sunny yard. "I'm sure Johnny never knew, either."

"Are you sure he's dead?" I had been flipping through the album, going back to pictures of Johnny as a baby, and then ahead to the last picture of him as a soldier, his red hair cut so short he was almost bald. "He couldn't be a prisoner over there somewhere?"

"Johnny was killed at the end of the war," Mrs. Russell said. "In a helicopter crash. He's buried here in Hyattsdale in Saint Phillip's Churchyard. Perhaps you and I could visit his grave one day, Tallahassee. I often take flowers from the garden, the ones he loved best. Marigolds, zinnias." Her voice trailed off, and we sat in silence, listening to a blue jay scolding from the dogwood tree in the backyard.

I turned back to the album, studying each page from beginning to end, watching Johnny grow from a baby to a man. He looked so happy in all the pictures, laughing and smiling, clowning around. It wasn't fair that he had gone off to a war and died so far away.

"You must miss him very much." I felt a big tear well up in one eye and splat down on the table cloth.

"Yes," she said. "It was a horrible war. My husband and I were very opposed to it, but when Johnny was drafted, he said he had to go." She paused and gazed at the picture of Johnny in his uniform.

"He was never afraid of anything," she said softly. "He told us not to worry, he'd be back home in no time."

I jumped up and ran to her side. Putting my arms around her, I hugged her hard. "But I'm here now," I whispered. "And I'll keep you company. Me and Bo."

Mrs. Russell's arms tightened around me. "I think I'll enjoy having a granddaughter, Tallahassee Higgins," she whispered.

*

While we were washing our glasses, Mrs. Russell said, "You must miss Liz."

"Not as much as I used to." I rubbed my glass hard with the dish towel, making it shine. "I haven't heard from her for so long. Right now I don't even know where she is, Mrs. Russell. Or if she's ever coming back. Sometimes I'm scared something awful has happened to her and other times I'm so mad at her that I don't even care."

I blinked to keep from crying. "I don't know what's the matter with me."

Mrs. Russell sighed and shook her head. "It's very difficult to understand someone like Liz. She's a complex person, Tallahassee. For instance, I've never understood why she ditched Johnny. He was crazy about her, and it almost broke his heart when she ran off."

She paused to let the water out of the sink. As it gurgled down the drain, she turned to me. "You know the way the sun bounces off something shiny and you see a little circle of light skipping around on the wall?"

"Like this?" I turned my spoon toward a square of sunshine on the counter and sent its reflection dancing across the ceiling.

"Well, you know you can't catch it," she said. "You can't hold on to it no matter how pretty it is."

I tried to cover the circle of light with my hand, but, of course, the second I moved the spoon, away the circle bounced.

"That's the way Liz is," Mrs. Russell said. "You can't hold on to her, you can't pin her down. All you can do is watch her dance away from you and hope she comes dancing back."

I shoved the spoon out of the sunlight. "But what's going to happen to me if she doesn't come back?"

"You're going to stay right here with your uncle and aunt," Mrs. Russell said. "And you're going to come see me as often as you like and give Bo wonderful, long runs in the park."

She put her arm around me again and gave me a big hug that almost squeezed the breath out of me. At the same time Bo jumped up and licked my nose. At that moment Hyattsdale didn't seem like such an awful place after all.

Chapter 22

ONE HOT DAY early in June, I came trailing home from school. It was Wednesday, so Jane was taking piano lessons and I was all by myself, thinking about what Mrs. Duffy had just told me. I was going to pass sixth grade, she said, but certainly not with honors. I was still doing very poorly in math, but at least I had turned in my homework and written a good report on Maryland history.

"If you would only pay attention in class," Mrs. Duffy had said as I was leaving. "This morning, for instance, I had to call on you three times in social studies. When I finally got your attention, you didn't even know what page we were on."

Although I didn't tell Mrs. Duffy, I wasn't interested in the imports and exports of South America. Instead of studying the map of Bolivia in our book, I'd been thinking about taking Bo to the park. I'd found a nice clearing in the woods where I could let him off the leash and throw sticks for him. While Bo dashed around,

I liked to pretend it was our own special enchanted forest, a place where anything could happen.

In my favorite daydream I found Johnny there, not dead after all. He'd tell me it had all been a mistake, somebody else's body was buried under that shiny pink stone in Saint Phillip's Churchyard. Then he would do a back flip and walk around the clearing on his hands, his long, red hair shining in the sunlight, while I cartwheeled after him.

At that moment Liz would appear. The two of them would rush into each other arms like a couple in a perfume commercial. Then the three of us would walk hand in hand (me in the middle) back to Mrs. Russell's house, with Bo leading the way. That was the best part — imagining the expression on Mrs. Russell's face when she saw Johnny.

Of course I knew Johnny would never come back. I'd never see him or hear him laugh, and we would never do gymnastics together. He had been in Vietnam before I was even born, and nothing on this earth would change that. But, still, it was more fun to think about the enchanted forest than to memorize the imports and exports of Bolivia.

As I turned the corner onto Oglethorpe, lost in my own thoughts, I noticed someone sitting on Uncle Dan's porch steps. Although her head was turned away from me, I knew at once who it was.

For a couple of seconds I stood still, my heart pumping as if I'd just run a mile. I had imagined this moment so often, I wasn't sure she was really there, and I wanted to look and look and look, just in case she was going to vanish the moment somebody interrupted my daydream. Then she turned her head and saw me.

"Liz!" I cried, "Liz!"

"Tallahassee!" Liz leapt to her feet and ran to meet me.

Then we were in each other's arms, and I didn't know where I stopped and she started. "Liz, Liz!" I burrowed into her. "I thought you were never coming back! I was scared you were gone forever!"

"You know I'd never leave you!" Pulling away, she looked at me. "Hey, let's see a big smile!"

I tried, but my mouth was all shaky. "Are you going to stay?" I clung to her, my mother, my Liz, the most beautiful mother in the world.

"You look great, honey. Thelma must be feeding you growth tablets or something." She tried to hold me at arm's length to see me better. "Has she been nice to you?"

"Not at first, but she's all right now most of the time."

"And Dan? I know he must be crazy about you."

"He's great, Liz. He fixed up your old bike for me to ride. He even painted it, so it looks almost new "

"That old clunker? It didn't even have gears." Liz laughed.

"It rides real good, Liz. You want to see?"

"No, no." She laughed and sat back down, flipping her hair over her shoulders. "I came to see you, not an old bicycle."

As I snuggled close to her, she shifted away from me

· 169

a little. "What are you trying to do, Talley? Sit in my lap?"

I blushed and let her put some distance between us. I'd forgotten how she felt about too much hugging and kissing. "Where have you been all this time?" I stared at her. "Why didn't you write me or call me? I've been so worried about you!"

"Oh, I've been just awful, haven't I, Talley?" She smiled at me like a little kid asking to be forgiven. "You must think I'm the most terrible mother in the world."

I shook my head so vigorously my hair flew out in all directions. "Of course I don't think that! You're the best mother, the very best in the whole wide world."

Liz tossed her head and laughed. "You sure are sweet, honey." She glanced over her shoulder at the house. "I've been sitting here at least an hour listening to that stupid dog bark. Does he always carry on like that? Or is it just me he doesn't like?"

I looked at Fritzi dancing up and down in the window. It was a wonder he didn't have laryngitis by now. "He's very excitable. Aunt Thelma says all little dogs are high-strung or something. That's why they bark so much."

"I bet Thelma trained him to be obnoxious. It's just the kind of thing she'd do," Liz said. "That dog even *looks* like her."

"He's not so bad once he gets to know you. He used to bark and growl at me all the time, but now he likes me. He only acts mean if I walk too close to his food dish. He doesn't want anybody near him when he's eating."

Liz lit a cigarette and exhaled slowly. "I never did care for little dogs," she said.

I waved the smoke away from my face. "Haven't you quit smoking yet? You know it's bad for you." I grabbed her upper arm. "And look how skinny you are. I bet you haven't been eating right."

"Who's the mother — you or me?" Liz laughed and pulled her arm away.

"Where's Bob?" I glanced at the empty street, thinking I might have overlooked his motorcycle.

Liz shrugged. "Oh, we split in California. As far as I know, he's still hanging out with those dumb friends of his. I was really wrong about him, Tallahassee."

She flicked an ash off her cigarette and surveyed the neighborhood. "Nothing has changed a bit here, you know that? I've been gone twelve years, and everything is exactly the same."

I looked at the street, softened now by the green leaves. Ever since I'd sat down beside her, I'd wanted to ask Liz about Johnny, but I hadn't had the courage to mention his name. She was the one person who could tell me what I wanted to know. Suppose her answer wasn't the one I wanted to hear?

While I watched Liz puffing away on her cigarette, I decided to ask her if she remembered Jane's mother. Then maybe I'd have the nerve to mention Johnny. "Do you remember Linda DeFlores?" I asked timidly.

"She still lives in the house behind us."

Liz looked puzzled. "Do you mean Linda *Barnes*?"

"Her name's DeFlores now." I frowned. "She says she used to know you."

"Linda married Bud DeFlores? With me out of the picture, I thought she'd marry good old Johnny Russell," Liz said.

"Johnny Russell?" I stared at Liz.

"Don't tell me you know *him*, too." She shook her head. "Lord, didn't anybody leave this place?"

Next door, Mr. Jenkins was running his power mower. The noise was making my head boom, and I couldn't think straight. "Johnny's dead," I blurted out, feeling my eyes fill with tears. "He was killed in Vietnam. Didn't you know that?"

Liz choked on her cigarette smoke and turned to me, her eyes wide. "Oh, my God," she whispered. "Oh, my God, no, Tallahassee." Hugging herself with her arms, she leaned forward, her hair hiding her face. "Nobody told me," she whispered. "Nobody told me!"

With her head on her knees she wept, her shoulders shaking. Timidly, I patted her back and stroked her hair, but she shrugged me away as if I were a gnat or something. I knew all the Fred and Ginger routines in the world wouldn't make her stop crying.

"I told him to burn his draft card," she said, "or go to Canada! Why didn't he listen to me?"

"Mrs. Russell said he wanted to go," I said. "She tried to make him go to Canada, too, but he wasn't scared of anything."

Liz shook her head. "When he got drafted, he laughed. He thought it would be a big adventure. I couldn't believe he was so stupid!" She buried her face in her hands. "I never even told him good-bye, I was so mad at him."

"Is that why you went to Florida? Because Johnny was going in the army?"

"That was part of it. I didn't want to see him when he came home from boot camp with all his hair cut off, wearing a uniform. It was against everything I believed in. Johnny a soldier!" She wiped her eyes with her fists. "How could he have gone over there?"

"Liz," I touched her bare arm. "I have to know something." My voice was shaking and my arms felt weak, but if I didn't ask now, I never would.

She looked at me, her eyes still full of tears. Then she turned her attention to the polish on her toenails, picking at a place where it was chipping.

"Was Johnny my father?"

While I waited for her to answer, Mr. Jenkins roared up and down the patch of lawn between his house and ours, filling the air with the sweet smell of cut grass. "Was he?" I felt my voice rising. "Was he?"

"You look just like him," she said. "You always have."

"But is he my father?"

"Yes," Liz whispered, "yes, and I'm sorry he's dead, Tallahassee. He would've loved you, he really would have. He was always crazy about little kids."

"Why didn't you tell me?"

"What was the point? I didn't want any ties to

· 173

Johnny, I didn't want to marry him or anything." She wiped her eyes again and lit another cigarette. "I wanted you to be all mine, my very own little baby. Just you and me forever like Peter Pan and Tinkerbell or something. Not that it would have made any difference, the way things turned out."

For a long time neither of us said a word. Fritzi had stopped barking, Mr. Jenkins had finished cutting his lawn, and the only sounds were the birds and the distant whoosh of traffic on Route One.

"Do the Russells still live here?" Liz asked finally. She had stopped crying, but she was pale under her tan, and her makeup was streaked.

"Mr. Russell died a long time ago, but Mrs. Russell is fine. She lets me play with her dog. You know, take him for walks and things. She likes me."

"Does she know that Johnny is your father?"

"She thinks he must have been. So I've been kind of like her granddaughter."

"I bet she hates me." Liz frowned, and I noticed the tiny lines on her face again.

"No, she doesn't," I said, "but I don't think Mrs. DeFlores likes you very much."

"I'm not surprised. It wasn't very nice of me to take Johnny away from her, but I couldn't help it if he liked me better." Liz didn't sound very sorry, and a little smile twitched the corners of her mouth. "So she's still living in Hyattsdale. And married to boring Bud. I bet she has a zillion kids, too."

"Six," I said. "Jane, the oldest one, is in my grade, and she's my best friend."

We talked for a while about school and how I was doing, but every time I asked Liz about herself, she shifted things around to me again.

"How about me and you?" I asked finally, unable to bear the uncertainty. "What are we going to do?"

"When do Thelma and Dan get home?" Liz looked up and down the street as if she expected to see them coming.

"Aunt Thelma should be here any minute, but Uncle Dan doesn't get home till five or five-thirty. They'll sure be surprised to see you."

Liz stood up. "Look, Talley, I don't want to see either one of them. I just stopped in to make sure you were okay, that's all."

"What do you mean?" I stared at her, bracing myself for bad news. "Aren't you taking me with you?"

"Not right now, honey." She backed away as I tried to reach for her. "I'm on my way to New York with a friend. He knows some people in the theater, and he thinks they'd be interested in me."

"But why can't I come?"

"You're better off here, at least till I get settled. You understand, don't you?" Her voice took on a pleading note. "New York's no place for a kid. You wouldn't have fun there, Talley."

I held myself very, very still. It wouldn't do any good to grab her, to cling to her. She'd only get mad. "Do you mean you're dumping me here? The same way you dump everybody?"

"What do you mean?" Liz stared at me.

"Johnny, Roger, Bob." I glared at her. "You even dumped our cat, Bilbo! And now you're doing it to me, your own daughter!"

"Don't talk to me like that, Tallahassee! I took care of you for twelve years, and don't think that was easy! A time comes when a person has to think about herself. I'm twenty-nine years old, and if I don't get into acting soon, it'll be too late."

"But you just said you wanted me to be all yours. You know, Peter Pan and Tinkerbell. What about that?"

"Oh, honey." Liz flung her arms around me and hugged me tight. "You like it here, don't you? Dan and Thelma take good care of you, you have friends, you even have a grandmother." She tried to laugh, but her eyes were worried. "Let's face it, I'm not exactly the world's best mother."

"You're the only one I have."

"Listen, I have to get out of here before Thelma comes home. You want to meet Max? Come on." She started walking down the sidewalk, almost running.

"No!" I yelled, "I don't want to meet Max! I just want you to stay here!"

She took a step toward me, hesitated, threw her arms up in the air and sighed. "I come all the way here just to see you and this is how you act! I can't believe it!"

Before she could say anything else, a little sports car

pulled up to the curb behind her. The top was down, and the guy driving it had long hair even though he was getting bald on top. "Are you ready, babe?"

Liz smiled at him, then turned back to me. "Come on, Talley, give me a kiss good-bye and say hi to Max." She stretched an arm toward me, beckoning, pleading.

I walked slowly toward her and let her introduce me to Max.

"This is Tallahassee," Liz said. "Isn't she the prettiest little girl you ever saw?"

"She looks more like your kid sister than your daughter," Max said as Liz hugged me.

I scowled at Max. "She's twenty-nine years old," I said. "And she's my mother."

"Kids, I love them." Max laughed. "You're a real trip," he said to me.

"Now you be good, Talley," Liz said. "This time I promise I'll write more."

I clung to her for a minute, breathing in the smell of tobacco and perfume. Then she pulled away and got into the car with Max. She waved and blew me a kiss, Max gunned the motor, and the little car sped away with Liz's hair streaming out behind it. I watched it turn the corner and almost collide with Aunt Thelma's car.

"Was that Liz?" she asked before she was even out of her old Ford.

I nodded. "She couldn't stay long," I whispered. "She's on her way to New York."

"You mean she left? She didn't even wait to see me?"

I shook my head and stared at a line of ants marching across the sidewalk. The lump in my throat was back, making it hard to talk.

"I can't believe it!" Aunt Thelma stared down the street in the direction the car had gone, as if she expected to see it coming back.

I didn't say anything, but a big tear splashed all the way down to the sidewalk like a drop of rain.

"But what about you? Did she say anything about sending for you?"

"Maybe in the fall," I whispered, "when she gets settled."

Aunt Thelma sniffed. "Well, we've heard that before, haven't we?"

Then she did something that really surprised me. She reached out and pulled me toward her, pressing my face against her bosom. "Oh, Talley, you must be so disappointed," she said as she patted my back. "I'm sorry."

I cried then, I couldn't help it. "She doesn't want me anymore," I told my aunt. "I'll never see her again. Never, never, never."

Giving me a huge hug, Aunt Thelma said, "Of course you'll see her again, Tallahassee. Don't be silly."

"No," I said. "She's gone forever this time, I know she is."

Aunt Thelma took my arm and led me into the house. "It might be a while, Tallahassee, but you mark my words. Liz will be back again."

Sitting me down at the kitchen table, she fixed us each a glass of iced tea. "Now you calm down, Tallahassee, and stop crying," she said firmly. "Tears aren't going to bring Liz back, you know that."

I sipped the cold tea, but it was hard to stop crying. After waiting all this time, I had just spent fifteen minutes with my mother. Not even half an hour. She could have at least stayed long enough to see Uncle Dan, to have supper with us. Jane could have come over and met her. Mrs. Russell, too. But no, she had to run off to New York with a creepy guy wearing an earring.

"Did Liz say what she's going to do in New York?" Aunt Thelma asked.

"That weird guy driving the car knows people in the theater," I mumbled. "She still thinks she's going to be an actress, but do you know what I think?"

Aunt Thelma looked up from her iced tea, waiting for me to go on.

"I think she's going to be a waitress all her life and she should have stayed in Florida. What will she do in a place like New York? She'll never meet anybody like Roger in a city."

Aunt Thelma patted my hand. "Well, Talley, I'll tell you something, I'm glad you're staying here. Believe it or not, I'd miss you if you went up to New York, and I'd worry about you all the time. The things that happen in cities — they're no place for kids."

"You mean you don't feel stuck with me?" This was surprising news. I knew Aunt Thelma and I were getting along better, but I never dreamed she'd miss me if I left.

She shook her head. "Not a bit." Then she stood up and went to the refrigerator. "Help me get dinner started now," she said. "Dan will be home soon, and I haven't done a thing."

As I pared the potatoes, Fritzi sniffed the floor at my feet, hoping something might come his way, and Aunt Thelma tuned in her favorite radio station. While she fried the chicken, she sang "I Left My Heart in San Francisco" with Tony Bennett, hitting a few false notes now and then as well as muffing the words more than once. From Jane's backyard I heard Matthew, Mark, and Luke playing some weird death-ray game they'd invented. I knew Mrs. DeFlores would soon shout at them to come in for dinner.

Maybe after we ate, I would go over and tell Jane about Liz's visit. She'd be furious at first, but then she'd dream up some wild explanation for my mother's behavior, and I'd feel better. At least for a while. But no matter what Jane said, I knew Liz and I would never live the way we used to. Too many things had happened. I had ties I hadn't had before. Mrs. Russell, my aunt and uncle, Jane. And so did Liz.

When Aunt Thelma wasn't looking, I handed Fritzi a little piece of the French bread I was preparing for dinner. "Here, greedy," I whispered as he snapped it up. "Me and you might as well be friends. It looks like I'm going to be here for a long time."